D0923501

MECHANICS' INSTITUTE
MECHANICS'
MERCANTILE LIBRARY

More advance praise for

Dick Scanlan's

DOES FREDDY DANCE

"A carefully composed, tautly executed debut collection of sixteen interlocking stories ... Austere, appealing surfaces conceal razor blades that, through Scanlan's graceful alchemy, defy rust. Stylish, relevant writing."

—KIRKUS REVIEWS

"Dick Scanlan's canny collection of memorable characters and engaging stories is a must-read. With his remarkably funny first novel, Scanlan joins the ranks of our most significant contemporary authors."

—ROBRT PELA, book critic for *The Advocate*

DOES FREDDY DANCE

by Dick Scanlan

Los Angeles ♦ Alyson Publications, Inc.

Cover design by Eric Kohler.

Typeset and printed in the United States of America.

Published by Alyson Publications, Inc.,
P.O. Box 4371, Los Angeles, California 90078.

This book is printed on acid-free, recycled paper.

First edition, first printing: September 1995

5 4 3 2 1

ISBN 1-55583-287-3

LIBRARY OF CONGRESS CATALOGING-IN-PUBLICATION DATA
Scanlan, Dick, 1960–
Does Freddy dance / by Dick Scanlan. — 1st ed.
p. cm.
ISBN 1-55583-287-3 (alk. paper)
1. New York (N.Y.)—Social life and customs—Fiction. 2. Gay men--New York (N.Y.)—Fiction. I. Title.
PS3569.C286D64 1995
813'.54—dc20 95-22003
CIP

CREDITS

"Cigarettes" appeared in *Christopher Street,* Issue 194, December 21, 1992.

"Gold" appeared in *Other Voices,* Vol. 7, No. 21, Fall 1994.

"Banking Hours" appeared in the *Antietam Review,* Spring 1993.

"The Clutch" appeared in *Other Voices,* Vol. 4, No. 13–14, Winter 1990–1991.

"Fallingwater" appeared in *Men's Style,* July–August 1995, and was excerpted in the *Mississippi Review,* Volume 18, Nos. 2 & 3.

"L'Attrape de Coeur" appeared in *Alaska Quarterly Review,* Spring/Summer 1995.

"Matinee" appeared in *Amelia,* Vol. 7, No. 3, 1994. Song lyrics are from "The Sun Has Got His Hat On" *(Me and My Girl,* lyrics by Ralph Butler, music by Noel Gray, 1937) and "My Favorite Things" *(The Sound of Music,* lyrics by Oscar Hammerstein II, music by Richard Rodgers, 1959).

The author wishes to thank Kendra C. Taylor, Eric Ashworth, and especially Edward Hibbert, agent/actor/friend extraordinaire, for their efforts on behalf of this book.

For Kees Chapman

CONTENTS

FAMILY ALBUM

Everyone was going to New York City except my mother and me. They loaded the light blue station wagon, arguing about who would sit where, my three brothers filling the very back seat with suitcases and my sister Katie handling the elegantly wrapped presents from Garfinkel's. This was not a store my mother usually shopped at, but she always bought special gifts for my father's parents, things she would never buy her parents, things she would never buy herself.

I'd gone with my mother to Garfinkel's, wandering into the fur department while she paid for her packages. The mannequins looked strange, mink stoles draped over their shoulders in the middle of August, but the store was heavily air-conditioned, and it made me forget it was summer outside, like being in the Penguin House at the zoo. This was before stores started chaining furs to the rack, animals in captivity, and I was able to wrap myself inside one of them, white and snowy and twice as long as I was. Even in the darkness the satin lining looked shiny, and pressed against my skin, it felt as cold and brittle as a thin sheet of ice. The fur muffled the sounds of shoppers, but I could hear my name being called over the loudspeaker as I waited for my mother's hurried footsteps and panicked voice to lure me out of hiding.

Dick Scanlan

My mother was relieved to see me step out of the coat, though when she recounted the incident to my father, he got angry, using it as proof that I was too young to go to New York. I suspected that he'd never intended to take me, that all along the plan had been for my mother and me to visit her parents in Nashville while the rest of them went north, staying with relatives I barely knew in the city I dreamed about. I considered being a stowaway, lying motionless under the Garfinkel's bags for however many hours it took to drive from Washington to New York, but when my father slammed the back door shut and called, "All aboard," it clearly meant all but me.

"Take care of your mother, Sport," he said, though there wasn't a sport I played well, or played at all unless forced to. "You'll have a wonderful visit with Granna, then we'll meet at the beach for a week of bodysurfing."

I said nothing. He knelt down, taking the thick cigar out of his mouth and whispering into my ear.

"There'll be other World's Fairs."

"When?" I asked, knowing my father had worked the last one in 1939, pulling a rickshaw to pay for law school.

"I'm not sure," he said, his hands on my shoulders, "but if you spend the next week moping, I'll never take you to New York."

"Don't be so hard on him," my mother said.

My father stood up. "Marge, he's too big to be acting like such a baby."

"He's only six," she told him, pulling me to her.

"I don't remember the other boys acting so..."

She must have made a face or shot him a look, because he stopped. He kissed her on the mouth, then kissed me on the cheek, and I brushed the wet spot where his lips touched my face, worried that he'd left a tobacco stain, like brown lipstick. My mother waved as the car pulled away, and I watched my family disappear, Michael and Katie waving, Chimp climbing over the suitcases. Paul had his learner's permit, but it was still strange to see him behind the wheel, my father on the passenger's side, his silver hair enveloped in a cloud of cigar smoke.

My mother finished packing for the trip to Tennessee while I waited by the window for our taxi, playing with my G.I. Joe, whose military uniforms I'd replaced with civilian clothes stolen from Katie's Ken doll. I was choosing his outfit for the plane when a car horn startled me, too loud for our suburban street, and as I drew the curtain, I hoped to see a bright yellow cab. Instead, I found an ordinary car, white and dirty, and riding inside it was another reminder of the New York sights I wouldn't see.

"We're making one stop before the airport," my mother told the driver, then looking at me, "Record Village."

The Village was my favorite shop, the next best thing to New York City, and my mother waited in the taxi while I went inside carrying a blank check with her signature.

The owner knew me from my weekly visits.

"Hi, Freddy," she said, smoke spilling out of her red lips as she spoke. "Going somewhere?"

"To Nashville," I said glumly. "How'd you know?"

She used her cigarette to indicate my carry-on bag, filled with my favorite albums, my smaller stuffed animals, and the formerly G.I. Joe wearing a Hawaiian shirt and chinos. I flipped through rows of records, no longer needing a footstool, now eye-level with the racks.

"Got the TV soundtrack to *Cinderella,"* she told me. "I set one aside for you."

"I bought it for my birthday. Remember?" It upset me that the owner of Record Village could not keep up with my collection. Already I had over twenty albums, Broadway shows and movie soundtracks, but I chose a pop album to take to Tennessee because I liked the cover, the Mamas and the Papas pictured together in a bathtub. The owner offered to fill out my mother's check, but I shook my head, having learned enough in kindergarten to write in the amounts of my purchases.

My mother carried my portable record player on board for me: she knew her parents didn't have one. Neither did my family until two Christmases before, when I told every Santa at every department store in the Washington area that I wanted a record player so I could listen to the one record my family owned, a 78 r.p.m. we called the "Family Album." It was recorded at our house on Thanksgiving, 1958, four months before I was born. My grandparents were visiting, and my father had hired an engineer to record the dinner conversation and press a record, though there was nothing to play it on. At one point during the meal I kicked, and though of course it couldn't be heard, I listened to everyone's reaction, my grandmother predicting that I was a girl, my father including me in his long toast to his loved ones. The Family Album was my first album, still my favorite, and I'd packed it in my carry-on bag, planning to play it for my grandparents.

▪ ▪ ▪ ▪

This was my first flight, and though I wished we were flying in the opposite direction, I stared out the window at the cars below, tiny like the Matchbox cars my brother played with. My mother had been on a plane once before and hated it, and she seemed tense, almost sick, asking the stewardess to look after me so my mother could close her eyes. I remember the stewardess's bun, bleached blonde and high on her head, and when we landed my mother took a picture of the stewardess and me on the runway.

My grandparents were waiting for us in the airport lounge. They looked uncomfortable, as if wary of air travel, my grandmother hunched over, her head almost facing the floor. She hugged my mother as my grandfather shook my hand. He was over a foot taller than my grandmother, his faded overalls emphasizing the length and leanness of his body. He opened his arms to embrace my mother, but she handed him my record player and walked past him, her one hand holding mine, her other arm linked with my grandmother's.

She hadn't seen her parents in two years, since our last trip to Tennessee. We'd driven down, all five children and my parents crowded into the station wagon for sixteen hours. My memories of that visit were vague: how long my grandmother's gray hair was when she let it down, how musty my grandfather's toolroom was. We left early one morning after a night of angry voices that had kept me awake, my father saying that Katie could have been ruined by my grandfather. I lay in bed wondering if ruined was the same as spoiled, if Granddaddy had given Katie too many gifts, the way my mother bought me whatever I wanted despite my father's protests.

For our arrival, my grandmother had baked me buttery cookies and southern-style blondies, so good I asked for seconds, then thirds.

"Sister," said my grandmother, an expression I recognized from the Family Album, "don't you feed this child?"

"Occasionally," my mother said. "I lost the joy of cooking after years of cleaning your kitchen." She'd also lost her southern accent, though her words still slurred after my father mixed martinis. Once I woke up from a bad dream and called for my mother in the middle of the night, but when she came to comfort me, I could barely understand her.

I carried a plate of cookies upstairs to the room I'd be staying in, setting up my record player and unpacking, my stuffed animals lined up along the large bed and Joe on top of the dresser. My grandfather came in with my suitcase, my mother and grandmother right behind him, and as my mother put my clothes away, my grandmother sat on the bed, her arm around my shoulder, asking me questions right off the Family Album.

"What do you want to be when you grow up?"

"I want to be a movie star," I said, ready with my answer, "and live in New York City."

"Movie stars live in Hollywood," said my grandfather, still standing in the doorway.

"What kind of movies do you want to make?" asked my grandmother.

"*Mary Poppins*," I said.

"But they've already made that movie, darlin'," my grandmother told me.

"I want to play the boy in *Mary Poppins,*" I repeated, and she laughed, ruffling my hair with her hand.

That night my grandparents had a cookout, their small backyard filled with relatives eating barbecued chicken. My mother sat at a picnic table with her two brothers, and though their wives wore makeup, pink circles and powder blue stripes, my mother was the beauty, with dark red hair and pale green eyes. I looked like my cousins, lanky and blond, but they all agreed I talked funny, "like a Yankee"; I didn't tell them that kids up North also laughed at the way I spoke. After dinner, we played hide-and-seek, and I was good at the hiding part even without a full-length fur, fitting myself into a kitchen cabinet, flattening myself under a bed. I didn't like being "it" though, the person who must find the hidden players, since it meant searching my grandfather's toolroom, which was dark and damp, with trays of metal nuts and bolts making it seem cold. Saws and hammers of various sizes hung on the wall, and behind his worktable I found dozens of liquor bottles, most of them empty but still reeking of whiskey, a few of them half-full.

I was tired by the time my grandmother tucked me into bed, fluffing my pillow, kissing me on the forehead. On her way out, she stopped at the dresser.

"Little boys don't play with dolls, darlin'," she said, picking up Joe.

"He's not a doll," I explained. "He's a G.I. Joe."

"Where's his uniform?"

"He's gone AWOL," I said. I didn't know what AWOL meant, but my father had once said this about Joe, and my mother had laughed for minutes.

My grandmother did not laugh.

"Don't be fresh, young man," she snapped. "He looks like a doll to me."

"I'm sorry, Granna," I said, though I had trouble getting the words out, unable to breathe.

"On or off?" she asked, referring to the light.

"Off," I whispered. "Please."

The next morning Joe was gone. I searched around, behind, and under the dresser, but he was gone. I went to my mother's adjoining room to report Joe missing, but she wasn't there, so I headed downstairs, stopped on the steps by tense voices coming from the kitchen.

"He acts like a little girl," my grandmother was saying.

"Leave him alone," said my mother.

"He's become a sissy child," my grandmother continued, "and, sister, if you don't do something about it..."

"That's enough," my mother told her, and though their conversation seemed finished, I tiptoed back to my room, playing the Mamas and the Papas record so quietly I had to press my ear against the speaker to hear the music.

■ ■ ■ ■

I went everywhere with my mother that week: dinners with her brothers, lunches with her friends, a trip to the Smoky Mountains to visit her college roommate who'd married a man rich enough to build a house with an elevator, which I rode up and down while they reminisced. My mother even brought me to the beauty parlor, which smelled like hairspray and heat, and I flipped through a movie magazine as she sat across from me, her head hidden in a dryer, unable to see, or hear over the roar of hot air. This was our last afternoon in Nashville, and on the way back to my grandparents', she stopped the car in front of an old, run-down house with too many cars jammed in the driveway and too many children playing in the yard.

"This is the house I grew up in," she told me. "Only it was much nicer then."

"Why did Granna and Granddaddy move?" I asked.

"I guess they wanted a bigger place," said my mother, "but I'm not sure. I'd met your father and left Tennessee years before that."

"Maybe Granddaddy wanted a house with a toolroom."

"He had a toolroom in this house," she said quietly. "He's always had a toolroom."

She started to turn the key in the ignition, but I stopped her with my hand.

"Mommy," I said, "Granna's kidnapped Joe."

"No, Freddy. He's just been misplaced, but I'll buy you another when we get home."

I was up early the next morning, my records and stuffed animals all packed and accounted for, Joe still missing in action. My grandmother made me a big breakfast of hominy grits, pancakes, bacon, and I was on my third helping when my mother tried to hurry me along.

"Finish up now, Freddy," she said. "We've got some errands to run before we leave."

"Why don't you do what you need to do and let him stay here," suggested my grandmother. "Lord knows when Granna will see her Freddy again."

"Can't you come for Thanksgiving?" I asked, hoping for another Family Album. My grandfather got up from the table and went down to his toolroom.

"Not this year," said my grandmother, "I don't think."

"You'll keep an eye on him?" my mother asked.

My grandmother nodded. "Of course."

"I won't be long," called my mother from the driveway.

"Take your time," my grandmother told her. "Now be off with you, sister."

Granna filled my plate with a fourth serving, which I tried to eat as she washed the dishes, her shoulders stooped so far forward that from the back she appeared headless. She asked me about my brothers, raising her voice to be heard over the running water. I wanted to ask her what she'd done with Joe, but the thought of it made my heart pound and my throat tighten. Neither of us heard my grandfather until my grandmother turned off the faucet.

"Freddy," he was saying, "c'mon down here."

"You come up here," my grandmother told him.

"I've got a surprise for Freddy," said Granddaddy, "but he has to come get it."

I carried my plate to the sink. My grandmother scraped the unfinished grits into the garbage, but she did not turn the tap and rinse the dish as I started down the stairs to Granddaddy's tool-room. He was standing at his worktable, directly underneath the single bulb that lit the room, the light shining on his bald head.

"Come over here, boy," he said, taking my hand and leading me to a tray piled high with screws, nails, rusty hinges. "Take your pick, Fred. Whatever you want."

"What have you got?" I asked.

"That I don't know, so dig your hands in. You might find a funny-looking button, or who knows, maybe a piece of gold."

I started sorting through the top layer of junk, holding a thimble up to the light to examine it closely.

"What would a boy need with a thimble?" he asked, and I put it back, reaching my hand deeper into the pile.

"That's it," said my grandfather. "Don't be afraid to get your hands dirty. You're bound to find something special."

I wondered if Joe was buried in the junk, digging both hands to the bottom of the tray. Cars wheels crunched on the gravel driveway outside as I felt around for Joe's familiar figure, finding nothing more interesting than an old-fashioned skeleton key.

"What's this for?" I said.

Upstairs the kitchen door slammed shut, but my grandfather paid no attention, kneeling down and holding the key between his face and mine.

"This unlocks a magic door," he said, and behind him, my mother appeared at the top of the stairs.

"Freddy?" she cried, rushing down the steps. My grandfather dropped the key as she grabbed me, carrying me upstairs in her arms. I couldn't remember the last time my mother had picked me up.

"Granddaddy was giving me a key," I explained, afraid I'd done something wrong.

"The door was open," my grandmother told her, and I wondered if she meant the magic door my grandfather had mentioned. "I was right here in the kitchen."

"You always were," my mother said, and my grandmother's hunched back seemed to straighten.

"Pull yourself together, Margaret."

I'd never heard my grandmother use my mother's full name, but my mother wasn't listening. She held me in her lap, rocking me back and forth. "It was a mistake to come here," she whispered. "I want to go home."

The stewardess on the flight back didn't have a blonde bun, but short hair and a short temper. I sat quietly in my seat as she poured my mother a martini from a miniature bottle, a tiny replica of the bottles on my father's bar. I asked my mother if I could keep it, rinsing the bottle out in the bathroom and dropping it into my carry-on bag. By the time we landed my carry-on bag was clinking, and I held it carefully so the four little bottles I'd collected during the flight wouldn't break.

■ ■ ■ ■

My mother had already loaded her car for our drive down to the beach when she woke me the next morning. Excited to see the rest of the family, she wanted to get an early start, but we'd been on the road for only a few minutes when she stopped at a toy store not far from our house. Holding my hand, she headed straight for the G.I. Joes. I picked out a bearded man and named him Christopher, and my mother led me two aisles down to the doll section.

"He needs some clothes," she said.

I modeled Chris and his new wardrobe for my mother, finally settling on his madras swimsuit with the terry-cloth top. We drove with the windows open, the sky a clear blue, and I didn't even wince when we passed the "New York, 250 miles" sign. We'd skipped breakfast, so we stopped for lunch at an outdoor restaurant, ordering hamburgers and french fries. The wind was strong, and we hadn't eaten much when both our burgers blew away, twirling through the air like UFOs. My mother managed to weigh the plate of fries down with her soda, but we were laughing so hard about the flying food, we nearly choked as we tried to eat them.

Slowly she drove down a side street of the small beach town, looking for the house they'd rented. It wasn't hard to find: my father had hung a big sign out front: "Welcome Mom and Freddy!" He came out of the house waving his cigar as we pulled into the driveway. The rest of my family appeared from different directions, Paul and Katie from the backyard, Michael's face in an upstairs window, Chimp climbing down from a tree. Inside, there was a large box with a red satin bow waiting for my mother on the dining room table, and oddly shaped presents for me. I could tell one of them was a record, and I saved it for last, opening an Empire State Building pennant from my brothers and the program to *Hello, Dolly!* from Katie. My father watched as I unwrapped the record, trying not to tear the cellophane.

"Music from the 1939 World's Fair," my mother read when I held the album up.

"That's one I know you don't have, Sport," said my father.

He held my hand as we walked the few blocks to the ocean, passing restaurants and bars. My mother had stayed behind to check out the house, so Katie held my other hand and my brothers walked ahead, eager to get one last swim before sunset. My father had his bathing suit on, but he did not go in, sitting with me on the shelf of sand the high tide had formed. We watched Katie and my brothers dive through waves, sometimes disappearing and resurfacing at our feet when they'd caught a wave at the right time.

I pointed straight ahead, toward the ocean.

"If I swam out to sea, I'd end up in..."

"Europe," answered my father. "You'd be swimming east, and you'd end up in a country called Spain."

"What's that?" I asked, pointing to the right.

"That's south, where Granna lives," he told me, then taking my hand and aiming it north, "and this is the way to New York City."

My sister and brothers burned that first day, spending the rest of the week with white lotion coating their noses and wet t-shirts in the ocean. I grew darker each day, the only one who tanned, sitting in the sun while my mother stayed under her umbrella, sunglasses covering her eyes, a beach towel draped over her legs. She said the sun tired her out, and I wondered if that's what caused the slurred words I heard from the front porch, late at night and long after I was supposed to have fallen asleep.

■ ■ ■ ■

The *World's Fair* record featured my father's most famous rickshaw passenger, Dorothy from *The Wizard of Oz*, singing "Over the Rainbow." I played it over and over again, and my father explained that though the record was new, the recording was made when he was young, a long time ago, so it had a tinny, crackling quality. The Family Album was only six years old, but with no cover for protection, it sounded worse than the *World's Fair*. I listened to it one night after dinner, and in the middle of my grandfather's conversation with Katie, I discovered a skip.

"You're the spitting image of your mama," said his voice on the record, "and every bit as purdy purdy purdy purdy..." It sounded like he had the hiccups, making Chimp and me laugh, but my mother was irritated.

"You're going to ruin the needle playing that old record," she told me.

Granddaddy's voice was still stuck on "purdy," and I could picture his face as he spoke.

"Please take it off," said my mother.

I started chanting along with my grandfather, "Purdy, purdy, purdy," and Chimp laughed even harder.

"I said TAKE IT OFF," my mother shouted, knocking the needle so it screeched across the album, leaving a long scratch. My father sent Chimp and me to separate rooms, and I lay on Paul's large bed, clutching Chris until I fell asleep.

When I awoke, Paul was sleeping beside me, and my father was leaning over him, trying to wake Paul up.

"Your mother's disappeared," my father told him. "We've got to find her."

"What?" Paul said groggily.

"Shhhh," whispered my father. "Don't wake Freddy."

"Where could she have gone?" asked Paul, stepping into his pants.

"I don't know. I must've fallen asleep on the porch. I woke up and she was gone. I've searched the house already."

I sat up when I heard them leave and thought of how I'd upset my mother, making fun of Granddaddy's voice on the Family Album. I pictured the ocean at night, black and dangerous, swallowing her up. Hours seemed to pass as I held Chris against my cheek, his pointed nose digging into my lip, but the glow of sunrise was nowhere in site when I heard heavy footsteps on the porch. The front door opened and I saw them pass by Paul's room and into my parents'.

"Get your hands off me," my mother was saying, one word slurring into the next. "Sister can undress herself." Her speech sounded so distorted that I wondered if they'd brought the wrong woman home.

It was my mother I found at breakfast the next morning. She'd already gone to the store, buying us fresh doughnuts and snacks which we took to the beach, and I sat under the umbrella with her as the rest of my family swam. I'd been in the ocean every day, riding waves on my father's back, but a storm was scheduled to hit Delaware that evening and he thought the water was too rough for me. Instead I played with Chris, his swimsuit on, his matching top off.

I left Chris lying in the sun to tan his plastic body as I walked to the edge of the water and waved at my family. They were too busy trying not to get dunked by the large waves to notice me walking north along the shore, stopping every few minutes to see if my mother was watching me. She was wearing her sunglasses, so I couldn't tell where she was looking, but as I got farther away, her umbrella became a small spot of red, and I realized she wasn't looking at me. Soon I was passing fewer and fewer people, and I could barely see my mother in the distance. Not that I turned around much: I kept my eyes forward, my feet moving toward the World's Fair and New York City.

The first raindrop fell heavy and weighted against my forehead. I didn't know how far I'd walked, but the boardwalk had ended and now just homes lined the beach. I continued north, wondering how long it would take to walk to New York, especially since it took at least a couple of hours to drive there. The ocean seemed angry and I moved away from it, afraid that one of its larger waves would knock me down and drag me under by the ankles. The sudden clouds had made the temperature drop, and I felt cold. What little I could see through the rain ahead of me did not look familiar, and I stopped to think about what I was leaving behind: Christopher, my record collection, my mother. I turned around and headed back toward my family, slowly at first, then running through the rain until the umbrella came into view.

Katie spotted me first. She and Paul ran to me, Paul scooping me in his arms and carrying me to shelter under my mother's umbrella.

"He must have gotten lost," Katie said as my mother wrapped me in the only towel not drenched from the storm. I said nothing. My father knelt next to me, his face gray, the color of wet sand.

"We found this," he said, holding Chris in his hands. "We didn't know what had happened. That big ocean..."

"Michael and Chimp went back to the house," Paul told me, "in case you'd gone there."

"Let's get you into some dry clothes, Sport," said my father, but when he stood up to leave, my mother held me closer. I looked up at her face. She wasn't wearing her sunglasses, and her blue eyes were filled with tears.

"It's okay, Marge," my father said. "Freddy's back." Gently he rested his hand on her shoulder, but she cried harder, making sounds, not words that I could understand, but shudders and sighs and short gasps of breath.

"Honey," he tried again. "Let's go. The rain..." She shook her head, and though it was pouring, he stopped. Katie was shivering, her colorful bikini showing underneath her wet, almost transparent sweatshirt. She and Paul and my father stood outside the umbrella, the rain whipping across their faces. My mother was weeping now, the wind carrying her cries away as I buried my face in the warm towel she'd wrapped around me.

Cigarettes

My brothers and I watch through our kitchen window as colonial-style furniture is lifted from a large moving van and carried inside the colonial-style house by mean-looking men. One of them sits on the back of the truck, sweat stains on his shirt, though all he's done today is blow a series of perfect smoke rings from the cigarette he's always smoking. He never looks in the direction of our window, yet I feel as if the rapid rings he blows like bubbles are for our benefit. My brothers laugh at his Elvis Presley hairstyle, but I've never seen anyone with slicked-back blond hair before. I watch him as my brothers identify two parents and a daughter. There is supposed to be a boy, but none of us sees anything resembling one.

My mother has gleaned some information about the boy from an unknown source. He is sixteen, one year older than my brother Michael, though the boy is reportedly in the same grade. This indicates problems at school, perhaps a failure, or maybe even expulsion, which interests my brothers and me. My mother also heard that he is adopted, which I pay particular attention to, since I've long fantasized that the redheaded, blue-eyed family I'm the youngest member of is not the real family of blond, brown-eyed me.

But the main reason we are interested in the arrival of the boy next door is where he's moving from: Sligo. My brothers have kept me awake nights telling me tales about Sligo. They've described the greasers and hoods who hang out in the woods that surround Sligo High, torturing children with lit cigarettes. I beg them to stop, and when they do, I beg them to tell me more. What they do with those lit cigarettes, where they put them.

My mother says we should introduce ourselves. "Go next door and say hello."

"He might carry a switchblade," says Chimp. He is thirteen, two years older than I.

"It's wrong to make assumptions about a person just because he comes from Sligo," says my mother. Even in her soft voice, "Sligo" sounds like a dirty word, something I'd be punished for saying, though I am rarely punished. I never get bad grades like Chimp. I never talk back to my father like Michael; I don't talk to my father much at all.

When the moving van leaves, Michael and Chimp go out to collect subscription money for their paper route and I go upstairs to my room. My picture window faces the woods behind our house, already lush with early spring leaves, but I can see the corner of my new neighbors' house through a small side window. The sheer curtains they've hung blur the activity inside, silhouetting the people, and I assume if I can't see them, they can't see me, so I pull my macramé out from under the mattress and stretch it along my bed. Eventually it will be a belt, but right now it's just a couple of knots and several feet of string. I am reviewing the instruction booklet, trying to figure out the next knot to tie, and though I'm aware of footsteps on the stairs, the knock on my door startles me.

"Just a minute," I say, but Michael and Chimp burst into the room before I can hide the macramé materials. They are with the Elvis Presley moving man from this morning, who Michael introduces as the boy next door. He leans against my doorway, still looking lazy, though the shirt is clean and the cigarette is gone, including the one he had tucked behind his ear like a white streak combed into his blond, greased-back hair. He looks shorter than he did sitting on the truck, not much taller than Michael, though something makes him seem older than sixteen, eighteen at least. Something more than his mustache makes him seem like a man.

"We collected over a hundred bucks," says Chimp, waving a wad of cash. He clears a spot on my desk, dividing the bills into ones, fives, and tens.

"Most of that goes to the *Post,* "Michael reminds him, standing behind Chimp and watching him count the money. The boy is watching me. His lips are slightly parted, and I almost expect to see smoke rings floating out of them when he speaks.

"You're the youngest?" he asks.

I nod. He moves into the room and sits on the edge of my bed. He has layers of smells, cigarettes covered up by soap covered up by a spicy scent that makes me hungry. I lean back against my pillows. The boy picks up one of the macramé strings and turns it into a noose, tightening it around his finger.

"How come you get your own room?" he says.

"I guess I'm special."

"I guess you're spoiled," says Michael, turning away from Chimp, trusting him to divvy up the money they've made this month.

The boy looks at Michael, then back at me. He is sort of smiling, though on his face it doesn't seem friendly, just a slight movement of his dirty-blond mustache. I check to see if he is wearing white socks, the traditional greaser's garb, but his socks are black and filmy, like the wings of a fly. His shirt is made of the same material, and I can see the glow of his skin underneath it.

"You got a cigarette?" the boy asks me, touching my arm with his strangled fingertip, which is blue now, and cold as ice. Chimp stops counting and I know we are both thinking of those Sligo stories.

"He's eleven," laughs Michael.

The boy shrugs. "I started in first grade, but I wasn't hooked till second." His blue eyes remain smoky and half-closed, but again he moves his mustache, holding it in a lifted position until the three of us laugh at what he said.

My bed feels much lighter when the boy stands up. I notice how slender he is, though broad shouldered, and I'm surprised. I remember being struck by his strength this morning the few times he chose to demonstrate it, and just now his weight seemed almost too great for my bed, as if gravity were pulling on him extra hard. I feel as if I'm being pulled, following the three of them into Michael and Chimp's room, which we call the Boys' Dorm, though there are two other males in the family: my oldest brother, six feet four since I can remember and very much a man, and myself. I try to emulate other boys, the way they walk, the way they throw, the way they run, but my attempts always fail, leaving my classmates disgusted and my brothers embarrassed by my girlishness.

The boy looks out the window, his back to us, his hands in his pockets.

"How far back do these woods go?" he asks without turning around.

"Fourteen acres," answers Chimp. I watch the boy's body for a reaction, wondering how our woods compare to Sligo High's.

"There's a park not too far from here," Michael says as he lays three piles of cash on his dresser: one for himself, a smaller pile for Chimp, a big pile for the *Washington Post*. "Want us to take you there?"

"Yeah," he mumbles, following Michael and Chimp. His spicy tobacco smell lingers in the air as he passes by.

"Hey," I whisper. The boy stops. I can hear my brothers stomping down the stairs. "Were you serious about the cigarette?"

"You do smoke?" he asks.

"My mother," I tell him. "She doesn't smoke, but she loves the smell of cigarettes, and she keeps some in her bathroom."

My brothers are calling us from downstairs. "I'm showing him my record collection," I scream down to them. "Be there in a minute."

"Get me a couple," the boy says, leaning against Michael's dresser.

I leave him in the Boys' Dorm and tiptoe through the master bedroom, into my parents' bathroom. Cigarettes are crammed into a cut-crystal glass, like toothpicks. I like the uniformity of them, the same length, the same width, the same brown tips of tobacco staring at the ceiling like eyes. I pull one out and they rearrange themselves, still packed tightly. Another would be risky, so I check the ceramic box that sits next to the soap dish and find more cigarettes, taking as many as I think I can without my mother noticing. When I come out of her room, the boy is standing at the top of the stairs. He says nothing when I hand him the five cigarettes. They disappear into his shirt pocket and he is at the bottom of the stairs before I've taken the first step.

By the time we get to the park, there are eight or nine of us, with nicknames like Shorty, Dude, and Lemons. They call themselves a gang, but not in front of the boy next door. He knows what a real gang does: he's from Sligo, and his presence at the playground makes them seem like a group of prep school boys during recess, some on swings, some on benches. Chimp takes over the jungle gym and I sit alone on a ride that goes around and around, but only if someone is sitting across from you, combining their weight with yours to make it happen.

I wait for the boy to smoke a stolen cigarette, but he doesn't. He lies along the sliding board for a while before sitting across from me and rocking back and forth to get things going. He drags his foot along the ground at first to make us circle slowly, but soon he picks his feet up and we begin to gather speed.

"What's the longest you've ever been on this thing?" he asks.

"I don't know," I tell him. His face is fixed in front of me as the park whirls around us. "Five minutes, maybe."

"Let's try for thirty," he says, checking his watch. I feel every shift of his weight. If he leans back, we slow down, though not much, and when he leans forward, we rush ahead, as if the ride is going to take off and send us twirling into space.

The other boys are gathered around, cheering us on, though they soon grow bored. At ten minutes many of them have left. My brothers seem to grow concerned when we hit the fifteen-minute mark.

"You're going to get sick," Michael warns me.

"I feel fine," I tell him, and I do. We are going around faster than I've ever gone before, but I feel like I'm standing still, staring at the boy as my brothers and the rest of the world rotate around me. I'm staring at his blond hair, no longer slicked back, but blown back by the wind.

At twenty minutes we are alone. Michael and Chimp have left, angry, though I'm not sure why, since I'm doing something daring, something no girl would do.

"Two minutes," the boy tells me, looking at his watch, holding on with one hand. I become aware of how tightly I'm gripping the handle, needing both my hands, all my strength to fight the centrifugal force that's trying to pull us apart.

The boy controls our slowing down, though when we've finally stopped, I still feel like I'm spinning. He jumps off and walks toward me, but I can't focus enough to know whether or not he's walking normally. Part of me wants to run from him, but I'm afraid if I stand up, my legs will give out.

They do. I lie on the ground, the cool, dry dirt feeling good against my skin. Above me the trees, the clouds, the houses in the distance look like they're flying, and the birds seem suspended in the air. The boy leans over and lifts me up, wrapping his strong arms around me and helping me walk. He is carrying almost my full weight, my feet barely touching the ground as we head back home through the woods.

We are almost there when he stops, sitting me on a tree stump and taking out one of the cigarettes. He strikes a wooden match against the bark of a tree and lights up, holding the cigarette to me. For a moment I think those Sligo stories are about to come true, and then I realize he is offering me a drag. I still feel sick from the circle ride, but I take a puff of the cigarette. The boy grimaces when I hand it back to him.

"You lipped it," he says, but he does not put it out. I watch him smoke the cigarette with the soggy filter. He keeps his mouth open, the blue smoke swirling inside like mist in a cave. It disappears with a sudden gasp and I wait for the smoke rings, but instead I see a pale gray stream that doesn't look or smell like tobacco smoke, more like a poisonous gas.

I leave him in the woods when I feel like I can walk.

"More cigarettes," he calls after me. "Tomorrow."

I don't respond, clutching trees to help steady myself as I climb through the woods and emerge in my backyard, where through an open window I hear my father's voice.

"When did you last see it?" he is shouting, and I'm sure he is talking to my mother, that they've discovered the missing cigarettes. My palm is sweating as I turn the back doorknob, but when I get inside I recognize Michael's voice, coming from the Boys' Dorm.

"I told you," Michael says, "two hours ago. Before we went to the park."

"And you're sure it was right here?" my father is asking as I climb the stairs. "You didn't tuck it away for safekeeping?" He is a criminal lawyer, and he sometimes treats us like clients who haven't given him the whole truth.

I try to slip by the Boys' Dorm unnoticed, but my father spots me and calls me inside. He uses his thick cigar to point at Michael's dresser, where there are now only two piles of paper-route money, the two smaller piles.

"Looks like a thief has moved in next door," my father tells me, and then asks us, "Was he alone in the room, even for a moment?"

"No," says Chimp, turning to me. "Unless you left him in here when Michael and I went downstairs."

I feel like I am spinning again. "I didn't," I tell him. "I brought him into my room. Showed him my records." I look at my father as I lie, but all I can picture is the boy, standing in almost the exact same spot while I went for the cigarettes. Beyond my father I see the woods through the window, and I search for a tiny orange dot, the glow of a stolen cigarette, wondering if the boy is still back there.

■ ■ ■ ■

I've been smuggling cigarettes to the boy next door all summer long, delivering the goods in a sandwich baggie. He calls when he's run out and I take as many as I can, but it's never enough to satisfy him. I assume he has other sources, maybe other boys who bring him cigarettes, and I wonder what his arrangement is with them, what these other boys get in exchange for stolen cigarettes. I get lessons on how to blow smoke rings, though it's been almost three months and I still can't blow one, tiny clouds of smoke escaping from my mouth whenever I try.

Today he gives his order in person. He knows we're going to the beach for two weeks, and he needs a surplus of cigarettes in my absence, concerned about the upcoming freeze on one of his supplies. He comes over in the morning under the guise of saying good-bye to Michael and Chimp, and I wait in my room, working on my macramé, knowing it's me the boy wants to talk to.

He slips into my room, quietly closing the door behind him.

"They think I'm in the john," he whispers, kneeling next to me. I can feel his breath on my face, and I can smell it too. It reeks of tobacco, but I like it, the way gasoline sometimes smells good to me. "When do you leave?"

"Tomorrow morning," I tell him. "Early."

"This afternoon then. As many as you can." He turns when he gets to my door and mouths the words "a pack," forming a small square with his fingers, as if we are playing charades.

He coaxes my brothers to come to the park, trying to clear the coast for me, though my parents are still downstairs and the moment the front door closes, I hear my father's voice.

"I don't like having that hoodlum in this house," he is saying. "I know a criminal mind when I spot one."

"He's adopted," says my mother, which seems to excuse a lot of the boy's behavior, including the money he stole, which my father paid the *Post,* never mentioning it to our new neighbors. I wonder what I could get away with if I were adopted: at least it might explain why I'm different from my brothers.

I lay my macramé on the floor, weaving the strings, tying the knots, and waiting for my parents to go to the store so I can get into their room. I work swiftly, trying to finish the belt today to wear on tomorrow's trip. No one will ask where the belt came from, but my mother will admire it, like the vest I crocheted last summer. She'll marvel at the craftsmanship without mentioning the craftsman.

My parents call upstairs to me when they're leaving. I remain in my room for several minutes after I hear the car pull away, in case they've left the list behind or forgotten their money. Once I'm sure they're gone, I move swiftly and silently down the hall, past the Boys' Dorm and into my parents' suite. I turn the light on in my mother's walk-in closet. I've never stolen directly from the carton before, but I know where she keeps it, next to the fully stocked sewing kit that my mother never uses. My heart is pounding though my hands are steady as I take the carton down from the top shelf and slide a pack of cigarettes out of the box.

I'm in the middle of my job when I hear the front door open. Quickly I put the carton back, but I don't know where to hide the cigarettes, since a pack would surely show in my pocket. I remember the boy next door demonstrating his shoplifting techniques, how he slips the goods into his pants. Dirty magazines, candy — he covers them all with an untucked shirt and walks out of the store. I suck in my stomach and lodge the pack of cigarettes in my underwear, the elastic waistband pinning the cellophane against my skin.

Michael and Chimp are in the kitchen when I get downstairs, back from the park without the boy, who I assume is waiting for me in the woods.

"I'm going for a walk," I say, aware of the crinkling sound the plastic cigarette wrapper makes each time I breathe. They are used to me spending hours alone in the woods, sometimes packing a lunch and having a picnic by myself, reading a book by the creek until the pages turn pink from the setting sun.

The woods are too dense for much light to penetrate this time of year. My house soon disappears behind a wall of trees, their branches intertwined, their leaves interwoven. It is cool along the path that runs by the creek, and dark enough to be early evening, though there are small, sporadic patches of sunlight. The boy is sitting in one, on the tree stump where we normally meet. His head is thrown back, as though he's tanning his face, and whatever he puts in his hair to slick it does not dull the color: it looks gold.

"Where's the stuff?" he asks as I approach, his eyes shut.

"Guess," I say.

I have his attention now, and I hold out my hands like a magician setting up a trick.

"Give me the O's," he tells me, Sligo slang for cigarettes.

"You have to find them." I move close to him, but he does not search my pockets or inspect my socks. Instead, he stares into my eyes, and I guess he finds the answer there, because he lifts up my shirt, his hand landing on the cigarettes without even looking. He laughs when the elastic from my underwear snaps against my skin as he removes the pack from my pants.

I watch him preparing the pack, wondering why he slaps it against the back of his wrist, carefully tearing the silver wrapper, then tossing it on the ground. The white paper burns away as he lights up, taking such a long drag that half the cigarette turns to ash. He flicks it on his faded blue jeans and the ashes land on one of the many patches. I notice there's a large hole that's yet to be covered, high up on his thigh.

He hands me the cigarette, which I've learned how not to lip. "Pucker," he says after I've inhaled. He drums his fingers against my cheeks, producing a series of small rings. I take another puff.

This time he does not offer his help. I position my lips and blow, but I am unable to shape the smoke at all.

He has the cigarette again, sucking in smoke till his cheeks are hollow, talking as he holds his breath.

"This is how you smoke grass," he says, sounding as if someone is strangling him.

He's told me a lot about drugs he's done: hash, angel dust, windowpane. He also boasts about cars he's stolen and houses he's robbed, and I used to think he was lying, until he threatened to call a bomb scare into my school. He said he might even bomb it. The next day, in the middle of a math quiz, the fire alarm went off. We put down our pencils, turned over our tests, and filed out of the building, and though everyone assumed it was a routine drill, I knew what was happening before the bomb squad arrived. Our teacher was concerned only about finishing the quiz, convinced the call was a crank, and we waited for almost two hours as they searched the school, but no bomb was found. Still, I was afraid when we went back inside, walking down the hall as if it were a minefield. There were already rumors about the identity of the caller, all of them wrong: somehow, the boy must have known I wouldn't say anything.

He is blowing rings of all sizes, some as small as a nickel, others almost as large as my head.

"It's all in the jaw," he tells me, placing my hands on his face so I can feel the jerking motion his jaw makes. I expect his skin to feel greasy, I guess because of his hair, but it is smooth and clean, warm from the sun. The sun has also lightened his lashes and made his mustache more blond, and though I remember my father saying he sees a police sketch whenever he looks at the boy, I think the boy is handsome.

We are on the second cigarette. I suck in as much smoke as I can, taking the boy's hands and lifting them to my face. He pulls away after my first attempted smoke ring.

"You look like you're chewing," he laughs, taking the cigarette from me.

"Let me try again," I say, reaching for the cigarette. He holds it over his head, out of my reach.

"What's the point?"

"Come on. I'm the one who took them." I try to grab the cigarette from him, but he is too fast for me, transferring it to his other hand, then back again when I jump at it from the other side. He is smiling, but I am angry now. "I stole the stupid O's," I snap. "Give me a drag."

"I'll give you what I want to give you," he tells me, grabbing my wrists as I go for the cigarette. He waits till I stop struggling, then loosens his grip. "Close your eyes if you want a puff."

I do. I smell the cigarette coming closer, suddenly afraid he's going to brand me with the hot ash, leaving the mark of Sligo somewhere on my skin. I open my eyes, but he covers them with his hand. I am about to cry out when I feel the filter sliding between my lips.

"Take a drag," he says. I've never smoked with my eyes closed before. It makes me so dizzy, I'm sure I would fall over if the boy weren't holding onto my shirt.

"It's just the slightest twitch of your jaw. A reflex," he whispers, "something you can't control." I don't think about blowing or shaping. I try not to move a muscle as I imagine the boy's fingers tapping against my cheeks.

"Look," says the boy, taking his hand from my eyes. Floating in front of me is a smoke ring, tiny and lopsided. It expands in size as it wafts through the air, growing large enough to grab onto as it rises up past the trees like a smoke signal. He holds the cigarette to my mouth and again I inhale. I'm afraid I won't be able to do it with my eyes open, but I blow ring after ring, most of them misshapen, a few of them nearly perfect. He gives me the thumbs-up sign, blowing rings of his own, large circles of smoke that my smaller efforts pass through, like a circus act.

The boy stands up, a smoke ring hanging over his head like a halo. He takes the last drag off the cigarette and flicks it into the creek, where it lands with a sizzle. He savors the smoke, holding it in for the longest time. Finally he exhales, covering my face in a cool stream, like dry ice. It makes me shiver.

"Later," he mumbles, sliding the pack into his pants and walking away.

"I'll be back in two weeks," I call after him. "I hope I don't forget."

He stops. "Forget what?"

I gesture to the smoke rings lingering in the air, puckering my lips the way he taught me. He comes back, his lips mirroring mine. He presses them against my cheek, brushing his mustache across my face, like a caterpillar crawling over my skin. When he reaches my lips, he slides his tongue into my mouth. It feels slimy and tastes bitter. My hand is pressed against the hole in his jeans, clenched in a fist, hard like his thigh muscle. I don't know how many minutes a kiss is supposed to last, one or four or maybe thirty, like the ride. I feel as if I can't breathe, and I wonder how long I can live without oxygen.

He pats me on the butt as he pulls away. I keep my eyes closed, listening to his footsteps stomping on dry twigs, breaking fallen branches as he heads toward his house. I'm afraid he'll come back, but mostly I'm afraid he won't.

When I open my eyes, the last ring has risen out of sight. The sky above has turned gray, as if all the smoke we sent up this afternoon has formed a large cloud, blocking the sun, and though I hear the low rumble of thunder in the distance, I am not frightened until lightning flashes through the woods, like someone has taken my picture, caught me in the act. I can't remember what I've learned about lightning, whether it's safer to seek shelter under a tree or stand in a clearing. I know it's safest to be indoors, so I'm dashing down the path, into my backyard, inside the house. My parents are turning on lights and closing windows, preparing for this summer storm, and I taste the boy's tongue as I mumble hello, still tasting him after I brush my teeth in the upstairs bathroom.

The belt is where I left it, abandoned on my bedroom floor, and I inspect the work I did earlier today. It looks sloppy, the knots loose and the edges uneven. I unravel the strings to the point where I started this morning, then farther, till the belt looks like it did last week. I go more slowly than usual, determined to make the macramé seamless, hoping no one will be able to discern which part was done when. I keep my eyes on the belt, my back to the window that looks out at the woods, but I can hear the rain falling through the trees and it soothes me, washing away what happened between me and the boy.

The storm passes quickly and the sun reappears, though it still sounds like it's raining in the woods, water dripping from the leaves to the ground below. The house is quiet and I concentrate on my work until I hear a faint rustling against my door, growing louder and turning into whispers that seem to blow the door open.

"Your mother and I want to talk to you," says my father, glaring at my macramé as if I'm doing something dirty.

"Let me," my mother says to him. She remains in the doorway. "Is there something you'd like to tell us?"

"About?" I ask.

"This afternoon," growls my father, the cigar in his mouth glowing a hot orange.

I keep my head down, staring at my macramé, afraid they'll find proof of the kiss on my face, my lips swollen or my tongue discolored, like when I'm sick. I wonder if someone saw us, someone hidden in the woods or perched up a tree. Or maybe the boy told, bragging to my brothers the way he brags to me about his crimes.

"I was in the woods."

"Doing what?" asks my mother. I shrug, wrapping a string around my finger.

"I'll tell you what," shouts my father. He picks up my belt and throws it against the wall. I'm ready for him to hurl names at me, like the boys at school, and I wonder which one he'll choose. "Smoking cigarettes! Cigarettes you stole from your mother."

I wait for more, but this seems to be the only charge against me. Relief floods my body, like on the day of the bomb scare when the final bell rang and I knew I wasn't going to blow up. I look at my mother, who is hugging herself.

"I couldn't help but notice the missing pack," she says, as if she's apologizing.

"You left the light on in your mother's closet," my father tells me, like Perry Mason informing the murderer of his crucial mistake. "Where is it? What's left of it..."

"I smoked them," I say, not wanting my parents to know anything about me and the boy.

"Twenty cigarettes?" says my mother. "By yourself?"

"Not all of them. I smoked a couple, maybe four, and they made me sick. I tossed the rest into the creek." She nods at my father as though they've gotten the truth, but he still seems suspicious. "I'll never do it again. I swear." I say this softly, more to myself than to them, thinking of the smuggling, the smoke rings, the boy.

"I'll see to that," says my father, unbuckling his belt. "It's not the smoking I'm punishing you for. When you're a little older, we can talk about that, man to man. I'll even give you one of my cigars." I watch the leather tip of his belt slither past loop after loop, like a snake. "But stealing. You'll never be old enough to get away with that in this house."

My father sentences me to ten strokes of his belt. I wonder how many I would've gotten if he knew what I really did in the woods. He positions me over the bed, knowing I'm unfamiliar with this procedure, and tells me to pull down my pants. It hurts much more than I thought it would, but otherwise fits the descriptions I've gotten from Michael and Chimp, including my mother's pleas for leniency and my father's firm refusals. My mother cries, but I don't, in case my brothers are listening, the snap of my father's belt echoing through the house like a whip.

My mother leaves before my father's finished, and he seems to hit me harder once she's gone, as if he's punishing me for acts I've yet to commit, acts we both suspect I will. I tighten my muscles, knowing that's when it hurts the most, hoping the memory of this will keep me from kissing the boy again. Somehow I lose count, thinking number ten is number nine, so it is over before I'm ready for it to be.

"I never thought you'd do anything to deserve this," says my father, as if it's a prize. I am sprawled out on my bed, lying next to my macramé, which I run through my fingers like a rosary. "The others maybe, but you've always been such a good boy."

He closes the door behind him when he leaves. Slowly I stand up, my pants around my ankles. I see my neighbors' house through the side window, and though I can't distinguish his features through their lacy curtains, I can tell which blurred figure is the boy. My buttocks are burning from the belt, but as I watch the boy's shadow, I know my father didn't hit me hard enough: the marks he left will fade without a trace. I imagine that a cigarette burn does something permanent, making the skin hard and shriveled, creating a ring of charred flesh that won't float away, leaving a scar that can't be gotten rid of, only covered up.

GOLD

My big brother is on the phone with his girlfriend. I am listening through the door, listening to them fight, the same way I listen to my parents battle when they've had too much to drink.

■ ■

I met her at my sister's high school graduation. So did Paul. I was about to become a teenager and he had just finished. We sat next to each other as we always did, though we were the furthest apart in age, with ten years, two brothers, and my sister between us. Paul surveyed the girls and I surveyed their dresses. We were a team.

A procession of Catholic girls entered the auditorium in long, lace gowns, the color of vanilla ice cream. They looked like brides. My sister walked solemnly down the aisle, a rose in her hand, a cross around her neck. Years later she would walk solemnly down another aisle holding a bouquet of roses, marrying a man I knew she didn't love, trying to get away from my parents.

Colleen was near the end of the line, where the girls grew tall like Paul was, like everyone said I was going to be. I remember her with a wreath of wildflowers in her shiny brown hair. And barefoot. But maybe that was another occasion, a picnic on my brother's birthday or an outdoor concert on a summer evening.

■ ■

"Get away from that door," says my father. "We don't eavesdrop in this family."

"Let him stay," Paul shouts from the other room.

My brother wins. I stay. My father goes back to the TV room, back to *Perry Como's Christmas Special,* back to his bourbon.

■ ■

Later that night, the three us walked together on the beach. The ocean, my playmate during the day, frightened me in the dark. I walked between them, holding their hands. I could feel their attraction to each other passing through me.

She told Paul and me that she had met us before at one of our sister's parties. Neither of us remembered it. She said she had watched me in the kitchen making hors d'oeuvres and dips from recipes in my Betty Crocker Recipe Card File, the one advertised on TV, giving Paul instructions on how to pour and when to whisk, as though I were a master chef. She remembered thinking what a special child I was.

"And what did you think of me?" Paul asked.

Colleen was silent, but I felt her answer in my body. My brother must have felt it too.

■ ■

I want to talk to her. I always want to talk to her. The rest of my family panics when she calls, screaming up to my brother's room, "Paul, it's Colleen on the phone long-distance from London. Hurry." Long-distance phone calls frighten them. They think it means bad news, but her calls don't frighten me: I think they're glamorous. If I can talk to London, I can certainly go to London. Someday.

This time they're right, though. This time it's bad news.

■ ■

I was the only child in the family without red hair. Mine was light brown, the kind that turns gold in the sun.

I was the only boy in the family who refused to play little league football. Or baseball. Or soccer.

I was the only one who sang, traveling with a portable record player and my Julie Andrews albums so I'd always have someone to sing with.

■ ■

We recreated the entire concert at Woodstock in my parents' backyard. I sang every part: Joe Cocker, Joan Baez, Jimi Hendrix. Colleen played the guitar and my brother played the 75,000 spectators, cheering wildly and holding up a lighted match when we finished.

She was of her era. Long straight hair, big brown eyes, beautiful without makeup. She wore flowing dresses with Indian prints, and a choker of gimp that I made for her. I made one for Paul, too. They vowed to wear them until their wedding day, when they would replace them with gold bands.

She was willowy and tan, tan in a way my redheaded, freckled family could never be.

My brother called her the sun.

■ ■

"Did you sleep with him?" he is asking her. "Oh God."

Oh God.

■ ■

I heard them making love once. I was in the room asleep, or so they thought.

"I want to make love to you all over," he whispered to her in a voice I barely recognized as my brother's.

I listened all night, mesmerized by the wetness of it. It sounded like the ocean, but it did not frighten me.

■ ■

My brother is angry now. I can't hear what he's saying, but he's speaking in the clipped, metallic tone he uses to say something cruel. I want to scream at him to stop it, the way she does when he calls me a sissy and tells me to toughen up.

■ ■

It was I who first called her the sun.

She'd sent me a watercolor of a sunrise she painted during her first semester at Smith. It was waiting for me one afternoon when I got home from school. My mother had the tubular package in her lap and a scotch in her hand.

"What is it?" she asked, unable to focus.

"A portrait of Colleen," I said.

"What are you talking about?" said my mother, squinting at the painting.

"Didn't you know? Colleen is the sun."

■ ■

"I knew you were lying," Paul is saying to her. "I knew when I read that letter."

■ ■

I try to imagine the man she has slept with. I picture him with dark hair and a beard. He is shorter than she is. He is not handsome like my brother. I see them lying together somewhere in the green English countryside, an American student and her British professor, making those same wet noises that she and my brother made.

■ ■

We went to a *Messiah* sing-along at the Kennedy Center when she was home from Smith for Christmas. The concert hall was filled with poinsettias, their pots wrapped in gold foil. Even the conductor was decorated, wearing a red satin bow tie.

We stood when it came time for the choruses. My brother did not read music, but Colleen and I could, sharing a poorly Xeroxed score that the usher had given us, like a hymnal, my boy soprano and her folk voice blending together.

I wanted to marry her when I grew up.

Or, I wanted to be her when I grew up.

■ ■

My mother comes up behind me.

"Let them have their privacy," she says. She is sober. She speaks quietly when she is sober. "I know how much you like Colleen."

"Love Colleen," I correct her.

"I know. Love her. But there are some things you are too young to understand."

"I understand," I say. "Do you?"

■ ■

My parents were always polite to her, the way they are when they really don't like a person.

"I don't trust her," my sister told me. "Everyone at school thought she was weird."

"Everyone at school thinks I'm weird," I said.

My sister did not respond.

■ ■

I auditioned for the seventh-grade talent show wearing my mother's old wig, red and wavy, and a purple dress my sister had long ago abandoned. I used the boys' lavatory as my dressing room, hiding in a stall, my ear pressed against the metal door as I waited to make an entrance when my name was called.

I sang "The Sound of Music" along with the record, though I could hear Julie Andrews only on the high notes: I could barely hear myself, everyone was laughing so hard.

■ ■

My brother is silent now. Colleen must be speaking. I wish I could know what she is saying, but the only voice I hear is my father's, coming from the kitchen.

"Marge, can I fix you a nightcap?"

I don't hear my mother's answer, but I'm sure she says yes.

■ ■

Three ninth graders burst into the bathroom as I was taking off my wig. They slammed me against the stall and tore the dress off my shoulders, slapping my face and pummeling my stomach until I lay on the cold tiles surrounded by my mother's wig, my sister's dress and the socks I'd used to stuff it with, the Scarecrow in *The Wizard of Oz* with the straw beaten out of him.

■ ■

I am not angry at her, could never be angry at her. Colleen listens to me even when I'm not speaking. She looks at whatever I want to show her: a poem I've written, a record I've bought, a macramé belt I've made.

■ ■

My mother never mentioned the missing wig, but my sister asked about her dress.

"Has anyone seen it?" she said, eyeing me suspiciously, the way she used to when one of her Barbie dolls disappeared.

I couldn't tell her about the audition. Only Colleen, omitting any details about my costume.

"It was terrible," I said. "They hated me."

"Well, they must be crazy. I love the way you sing."

■ ■

"Don't say you love me," Paul screams into the phone. "You don't. You couldn't."

This makes me want to cry, because I know he is wrong.

■ ■

Her mother had us all over for an Easter egg hunt. She was a slim woman with black hair, a tan face, pink lipstick. I sat next to her at dinner, pretending she was Jackie Kennedy. We discussed J.D. Salinger.

"I'm in love with your youngest, Marge," she told my mother.

"Isn't he great?" said my mother in the loud Southern accent she had when she was drunk. "Did you know he was an accident?"

"Marge, please," my father said, trying to stop her.

"We meant to quit at four, but I'm glad we didn't. He's my favorite..." Her voice grew weepy, trailing off as her napkin slipped out of her hand and floated to the floor.

The only sounds I heard for the next several minutes were knives scraping against plates and ice cubes tinkling. Everyone was looking down. Except Colleen. She was looking at me.

■ ■

Paul's voice sounds younger than mine. "How can I trust you after this? How can I touch you?"

■ ■

I had not known I was unplanned. I did know that my parents weren't married when my mother became pregnant with Paul. I pieced it together from my grandmother's diaries, old snapshots, old letters. None of the other children knew this, though they had found the same diaries, seen the same snapshots, read the same letters.

I told Paul in my parents' kitchen late one summer night, soon after Colleen came home from Smith. I presented the evidence to him like the lawyer my father was, like the lawyer Paul would become. It was all there, my parents' real wedding date, their flight from the small Catholic college they were both teaching at to a city where nobody knew them, my grandmother's fear that my grandfather would never forgive the man who had done this to his daughter.

■ ■

He hangs up the phone. I hear glass shattering, probably her picture. He always destroys something valuable when he's upset.

■ ■

Paul was silent for a moment when I finished. He stood up, grabbed me by the collar, and slammed me up against the wall, wrapping his large hands around my neck so tightly I could barely breathe.

"If you ever show me this again, I'll kill you. Do you understand, I'LL KILL YOU," he screamed, banging my head against the wall until Colleen pulled him off me.

The house shook when he slammed his bedroom door. I heard it quietly open and shut again as Colleen slipped into his room, leaving me alone in the kitchen, trembling all over.

■ ■

There is no sound now but his tears, the wetness of his tears. It frightens me.

■ ■

I didn't cry until dawn, when I woke up on the living room sofa. Colleen was covering me with a blanket and putting a pillow under my head.

"You shouldn't have done that," she said. "You hurt him so much."

"I'm sorry, Colleen. God, I'm sorry."

"I know you are. And so does he. Now sleep."

"Colleen," I whispered after her as she tiptoed up the stairs, "I love you." But I couldn't get any words out.

"I love you too," she said, coming back, taking me in her arms and stroking my hair as I sobbed. She smelled warm and womanly, like an ocean breeze on a hot summer day. I fell asleep in the stillness of her arms.

■ ■

Paul calls out to my father. I have never heard him do this before. Even my father seems surprised.

"Coming, son," he says as he freshens his drink.

I wonder who Colleen calls out to. I hope her British professor is there to comfort her. I hope he takes her out to a pub for fish and chips and dark beer, like she described in her letter to me.

■ ■

I hadn't tasted fresh cherries until I met her. Or raspberries. Or honeydew melon. She told my parents she would drive me to school one morning and took me canoeing along the canal instead. We stopped at a farmers' market along the way where Colleen bought every fruit I hadn't tried. The farmers thought we were brother and sister. I wanted us to be.

■ ■

I go to my room and look at the letters she sent me. Her handwriting is bold, like an artist's signature, her stationery blue and fragile as tissue paper. Colleen writes postcards addressed to the entire family, but I get letters. I have read them so many times I have them memorized. Even the stamps. Even the postmarks.

■ ■

She mentioned a professor in one of her letters, an art history teacher who showed her around London. He took her to Charles Dickens's house, where she bought a deck of cards with the characters from *Oliver Twist* printed on them. She sent them to me long before Christmas, long before my birthday. They were gold around the edges. I didn't let anyone in my family touch them, not even Paul.

■ ■

I hear my sister and my mother talking in my parents' bedroom.

"Everyone at school thought she was weird," says my sister, her line on Colleen.

"I wouldn't be surprised if her classmates at Smith thought worse than that," my mother says in a confidential tone. "Girls like her always get a reputation."

I wonder if my mother got one.

■ ■

We were sitting in a bar on the boardwalk, my brother swigging beer from a porcelain mug, Colleen sipping Sangria, and me nursing a Shirley Temple.

"Is this what a pub is like?" I asked her.

"I'll let you know when I get there," she said.

I heard a loud voice coming through the door, a voice I recognized, though I couldn't place from where. It was the voice of my mother, drunk, stumbling into the room with my father and a group of their friends.

■ ■

The front door closes. I look out my window and see my father and Paul walking together, my father's arm around Paul's shoulder. My brother is carrying a bottle of beer despite the coldness of this December night. He isn't wearing gloves. His hands must be numb.

It is so cold I can see their breath as they talk. I can't imagine talking with my father.

■ ■

My parents laughed when they saw us at the bar, my father ordering a round of drinks for everyone. My mother hugged me tight, the way she does when she's drunk, so tight I could barely breathe. My face was crushed against her breast, her diamond brooch digging into my ear.

"Stay with us, honey," she told me when Paul and Colleen got up to leave. "Daddy and I will take you to that club I was telling you about, the one that has Julie Andrews on the jukebox. Let Paul and Colleen have some time alone."

"Don't worry about us, Mrs. Donovan," said Colleen, though she was looking at me.

"I think I'll go with Colleen, Mom. With Colleen and Paul."

My mother held me a moment longer, then kissed Paul on the cheek. She grabbed Colleen's hand, holding it in her firm, drunken grip. "My sons are so fond you, dear," my mother told her. "We're all so fond of you."

■ ■

I watch them walk around our large circular driveway. Round and round they go, past the hedges with the Christmas lights, past the mailbox decorated with pinecones and red ribbon, back to the front door, which is covered with gold foil and a huge wreath, like a beautifully wrapped Christmas present.

Colleen's gift to me is sitting under the tree, waiting for Christmas morning. We had plans to open our presents at the same time during a transatlantic Christmas phone call.

■ ■

My brother and I went to the airport to see her off. Her mother, Jackie Kennedy, taught me how to say, "Bon Voyage!" We waited until the plane took off, as people used to wait, waving goodbye from a large observation window.

Paul cried. Quietly.

I didn't. I missed her already, but I was filled with excitement, as though I were winging my way across the ocean for a year abroad, not driving back to my parents' house.

■ ■

The house is still. When my parents and my brothers and my sister finally go to bed, it is still. And always cold.

I tiptoe downstairs to the living room, where the Christmas tree is. The lights are on, which means my parents got drunk after Paul went to sleep and forgot to turn them off.

I sit on the sofa, staring at the tree, holding Colleen's gift in my hands. The package is dented, a corner of its red-and-white wrapping paper torn from the long journey overseas, but it is here in my hands.

■ ■

"We bumped into Paul's old girlfriend a few months ago at an embassy party," my brother's second wife told me when I was down from New York for my brief yearly visit. "She asked about you."

"How is she?" I asked.

"Fine," said Paul. "Married to a Frenchman."

"She's not that pretty," his wife said, and I could tell by the way she said it that Colleen was still beautiful.

■ ■

I open it slowly, carefully removing the red bow and setting it aside, as though it's the first — or last — gift I will ever receive.

It is the score to Handel's *Messiah,* an antique score bound in gleaming mahogany leather with my initials embossed in gold in the lower right-hand corner. It feels smooth. It smells expensive. Inside the pages are thick and cream-colored, with illustrations of angels, stars, the moon, the sun.

I turn to the "Hallelujah" chorus and start to sing, quietly of course, so no one in my house will hear me, though inside I am singing as loudly as I can. Inside I am singing with Colleen.

BANKING HOURS

I'd never had what my father called a real job in a real office, but now that I was a high school graduate, he insisted I earn some real money to put toward my tuition at the University of Maryland, so he got me a job at the bank. I had worked in a theatre since I was thirteen, selling tickets, ushering, one summer even acting. I wanted to study drama in New York City, at Juilliard or NYU, but my father felt that seventeen was too young to leave home.

"Two years at Maryland and we'll talk about New York," he told me, puffing on a thick cigar. "After all, Freddy, you're the one who wanted to graduate a year early."

My parents took my early graduation personally, as though I was trying to get away from them. I was the last child left, and spent most of my time in my room while they poured themselves "one more drink before dinner" long after I'd made myself a meal, soup and a sandwich. The next morning when I carried my dinner tray downstairs to exchange it for breakfast, my parents would be passed out on perpendicular sofas, wearing last night's clothes. The living room reeked of stale cigar smoke, and their half-drunk glasses of scotch looked like urine samples.

He was the man with the money, though, a successful attorney, and if I wanted to get to New York City it would be he who paid for it, just as he paid for my three brothers' and one sister's college educations before mine. If it meant working at a bank and spending two years at a university whose most famous theatrical alumnus was Ernest Borgnine, that's what I would do.

I told myself this as my father drove me to the bank that first day. He was meticulously dressed in a silver-gray summer suit, the color of his hair, the color of his cigar smoke in the morning sun. He never looked hung over, though he must have been. We rode in silence as we had during the single season I played Little League football as a favor to my father. Although my mother drove me to singing lessons and play rehearsals, it was my father who took me to football practice on chilly autumn mornings, my shoulder pads, helmet, and cleats in my lap, cumbersome and cold, like chunks of ice. The heater in the station wagon never worked, and my breath was as visible as the smoke from his cigar.

I was a better bank teller than a football player. The job lacked the glamour of theatre, but to my surprise, I enjoyed getting paid to work with numbers. There was one right and many wrong answers for each transaction, and all employees were bonded, insured, so if I chose a wrong answer, no matter how wrong, the bank would be reimbursed. Though the days were sometimes dull, the bank was comfortable, its temperature controlled, its walls freshly painted, its floors covered in emerald green carpet, plush compared to the cold sterility of my high school and the shabby disrepair of my parents' once-impressive home. Even the little compartments on the counters where the deposit and withdrawal slips were kept appealed to me: everything had its place, including me, but it wasn't a place I wanted to stay in for long.

From the beginning I was a big hit at the bank, though I had nothing in common with the other tellers: I was the youngest "on the line," as they called it. Charles, only two years older, already spoke of his high school wistfully, the best years of his life, and his long fingernails were stained yellow from chain-smoking.

Next on the line was Happy Ho, a Vietnamese woman, barely as tall as the counter we worked behind. She moonlighted at a nearby 7-Eleven, selling a cherry-flavored ice drink called a "Slurpee." Happy was serious, and Dixie, our head teller and my biggest fan, told me they'd never seen Happy smile till I started working there.

"Personality-plus," Dixie used to call me, rolling her big, brown, blue-eyeshadowed eyes and coating her bleached coif with hairspray. She was my immediate supervisor, the one I reported to every morning, always late, no matter how early I'd tried to rouse my father off the couch.

Dixie never docked me for my tardiness: I made her laugh. Stepping out of the silence of my father's smoke-filled car and into the bank was like stepping onto a sitcom, security cameras hidden in the ceiling to film my show. I'd do imitations of angry customers, of Mr. Mulgrew, the bank president with a thick Irish brogue though he grew up near Pittsburgh. My most popular impression was of our branch manager, Nelva, who came from rural Maryland and spent all day on the phone telling her husband, Big Kenny, that he couldn't go to the cockfights.

"Life's been a ball since Freddy bounced into this bank," Dixie would say, her cigarette waving up and down between her painted pink lips like a conductor's baton as we counted stacks of crisp new bills, called "clean" money though it coated our fingertips with black ink.

My show ended when my father picked me up from work. I would wait for him long after the bank closed, glad the other tellers weren't there to see me sitting on the curb, watching for his big blue car, like a furloughed prisoner waiting to return to jail. My driver's license had been suspended after four speeding tickets and one failure-to-yield-right-of-way. At the Traffic Court hearing, my father refused to defend me.

"Maybe now you won't be in such a hurry," he said.

Hurry or not, I had no license until September, though sometimes I drove home from the bank if my father had had too many "drinks before dinner" at lunch, weaving his way through the parking lot, turning the wheel over to me. I never asked him about his work: he always asked about mine.

"How was the bank today, Freddy?"

"Don't ask how the bank is," I told him. "The bank isn't."

"Isn't what?" he asked.

"Isn't anywhere I want to be."

I was afraid if he knew I liked the bank, he'd never pay for New York, so I didn't discuss the tellers, or do my bubble-blowing Dixie bit, or imitate Nelva screaming into the phone, "Naw, Big Kinny, ya cain't go ta dem cockfights." Nor did I tell my father I'd been named "Teller of the Month" for June, a monthly award given to the teller whose drawer came closest to balancing, which mine did every day, to the penny, making Dixie nervous.

"They expect you to make mistakes," she warned me, "a few cents here and there. It looks unnatural if you don't."

Still, she cried when Mr. Mulgrew announced my name, rolling the "r" in Freddy. I expected applause, but instead, I got snapping fingers, a bank tradition. Everyone snapped, even the bank officers in their dark suits, and it sounded like a roomful of popping popcorn as Mr. Mulgrew handed me a small badge, which Dixie made me wear under my name tag, proud that someone on her line had a perfect record. Mulgrew was a friend of my father's, the connection that got me the job, but he never told my father I was "Teller of the Month," and I kept the badge in my pocket during the silent rides to and from the bank.

■ ■ ■ ■

I'd been at the bank for over a month when Mandy came back. She'd spent three years on the line without missing a day until her miscarriage before I started. She hadn't wanted to come back: she was embarrassed because she didn't know who the father was, Dixie told me. Dixie told everybody everything.

I assumed it was Mandy when I walked into the employees' lounge, for once on time, and saw her talking with Charles and

Happy Ho. She had pale blonde hair that rested in soft curls on her shoulders, and her face was round and flat, with a button nose and Kewpie-doll lips. Only two of her features were sharp: her green, almond-shaped eyes, and her fingernails, long and blood red, a shocking end to her delicate, porcelain white hands.

Charles introduced us.

"Teller of the Month." Happy pointed to my badge.

"The first celebrity I've had the honor of working with," said Mandy, snapping her fingers.

Mandy's drawer was next to mine, and whenever a customer commented on my button, I would hear her snapping and giggling, so I started to snap when the regulars welcomed her back. Soon we were snapping when Charles talked about his beloved high school, or Dixie displayed another Avon product, or Happy Ho said anything at all. We kept our hands at our sides, snapping quietly so no one noticed, trying not to laugh as I performed for Mandy, capturing the customers' accents, their odd methods of handling money. When it was slow, we turned our chairs toward each other and talked.

"Why are you working at a bank?" she asked me during a lull between the lunchtime lines and the rush before closing. "I love having you here, but there are so many things you could be doing."

"You too," I said.

"I guess," said Mandy. "I just don't know what they are yet."

"I know what I want to do," I said. Charles stared at the clock and smoked, Dixie studied a Mary Kay Cosmetics catalogue, and Happy concentrated on a Vietnamese crossword puzzle while I told Mandy my plan to move to New York to be an actor.

"Not an actor," she said. "A comedian. That's what you should be. What are you waiting for?"

Mandy hadn't waited for anything. She'd left home after high school, saying good-bye to West Virginia and her family's trailer home and renting a small apartment in Rockville. She was saving money for her uncertain future and dating a few men when one of them got her pregnant. I sensed none of the embarrassment Dixie had described: Mandy seemed proud as she talked about the doctor's visits, the daily changes in her body, the decision not to have an abortion. Looking at her tiny waist, it was hard to imagine her six months pregnant, working on the line in maternity clothes, as she had been the day she collapsed.

Dixie was right: Mandy hadn't wanted to come back to the bank. She hated the way the customers looked at her, relieved that she'd lost the baby, as if a child might have ruined her life. The future she'd been saving for hadn't included a miscarriage, and Mandy ran out of money. She still had doctors' bills that insurance wouldn't cover, several hundred dollars' worth.

Mandy and I gossiped as much as Dixie did, whispering to each other as we set up our drawers in the morning, counting the coins and speculating about Dixie's real hair color, Happy's out-of-work husband, Charles's sexuality.

"He's been wondering about yours, too," Mandy told me. "I overheard him talking to Dixie."

I wasn't sure about myself, though my high school classmates were convinced I was gay. They cornered me in the locker room and slapped me with wet towels that sounded like cracking whips and left red marks on my skin. Other men had cornered me too: older men in mall bathrooms, an actor in a backstage dressing room. The only sound then was my zipper being pulled down as he slid his hand into my pants, my heart pounding when he made me feel him, bigger and harder than I was.

These were things I never discussed, especially not with Mandy, the first woman I'd felt sexually attracted to. Working next to her, I could smell her floral-scented shampoo, as though she'd just stepped out of the shower, and I imagined running my fingers through her wet, golden hair, and kissing her delicate neck as she giggled in my ear.

I didn't want her wondering about me, so I told her, "I hope you set Charles straight."

"I don't think that's possible," she said, and we laughed.

"Pay attention to your money and save the coffee klatch for later," Dixie would say every morning. "That's how mistakes happen."

Most mornings I was too late to talk, and once I arrived almost an hour after opening, angry at my father for sleeping so late and holding him responsible for every red light and stop sign along the way.

"Nelva wants to see you as soon she's off the phone with Big Kenny," Dixie said.

Mandy helped me set up my drawer, which she wasn't supposed to do. I told her why I was late, and told her about my parents' drinking.

"So move to New York," she told me. "You don't want to go to the University of Maryland anyway."

"On what?" I asked, waving a wad of fives. "A bank loan?"

"Start saving, Freddy. You don't need much."

"Do you know what Juilliard's tuition is?" I said.

"You don't have to go to college," said Mandy.

"And what would I do when I got to New York City?"

"Go there first and then find out."

I looked at Charles, already on his third cup of coffee and seventh cigarette at nine a.m., and Happy, cashing paychecks for people who made more in a week than she did in a month working two jobs. Even Mandy, whose eyes always flashed with new ideas, had nothing to fall back on but the bank. I had my father: if Nelva fired me for being late, my father could get Mulgrew to rehire me, or get me another job. I felt the protection of my father's prestige and my father's money as I knocked on Nelva's door, though I soon realized she wasn't going to fire me for being late, merely lecturing me on punctuality, a lecture I performed for everyone on the line, complete with her speaker-phone refusal to let Big Kenny go to the cockfights.

■ ■ ■ ■

The "Teller of the Month" ceremony was held at the previous winner's branch, so we hosted the July meeting. Happy Ho had left to sell Slurpees, but the rest of us sat together like the home team at a high school football game as tellers from six other branches filled the folding chairs. Mr. Mulgrew started his speech with "Top of the afternoon to you," and I took off my badge, ready to turn it over to the next winner.

"It's yours to keep," Dixie told me. "You'll always have been 'Teller of the Month' for June."

The snapping started when Mulgrew announced the winning name, an older woman wearing a gold brooch with the bank's logo, surrounded by three "Teller of the Month" buttons.

"I don't know where to put it," she said as Mulgrew handed her the badge.

"I have a suggestion," I whispered to Mandy, and we laughed as clicking fingers swelled to an ovation.

At the reception afterwards, with store-bought cookies and canned punch, the employees were supposed to mingle, but each branch formed its own group, seven tiny circles scattered throughout the room. I introduced Mandy to Mr. Mulgrew, who'd never known her name.

"Nice to meet you, lassie," he said, winking at me man-to-man.

Mandy and I had agreed to be the cleanup committee, collecting empty glasses and half-eaten cookies. We took our time folding up chairs, stacking them in the storage closet, but I still had over an hour's wait before my father picked me up.

"I'll drive you home," Mandy offered.

"You live in the opposite direction," I said.

"Yeah," she giggled, "the other side of the tracks."

I left word with my father's secretary, then followed Mandy to her car, an orange VW filled with mismatched shoes and last month's magazines. She was used to driving alone: the passenger's seat was cluttered with soda cans and candy wrappers, which she tossed onto the floor, clearing a place for me. It was an adventure for both of us, me riding too fast in her funky car and her driving through increasingly exclusive neighborhoods, but as the homes got bigger, the gardens well kept, Mandy grew quiet, as if the gap between us was as wide as the space between the houses we were passing. By the time she pulled into my circular driveway, we were silent. She kept the motor running as she stared at my parents' huge white house set back amidst hundreds of trees.

"You live here?"

"Until I move to New York," I said. "I'd ask you in, but..."

"I understand," she said.

As she drove away, I wondered if she understood that it was I who was embarrassed, by the stack of unwashed breakfast dishes, the empty bourbon bottles on my father's bar, my mother sitting drunk in the darkened living room.

The sun set outside my bedroom window, replaced by a bright moon that shone on the trees below, and in my mind I turned those tall trees into tall buildings, all glass and steel, lit up at night like the New York skyline. I remembered Mandy telling me that her one-room apartment faced a brick wall, and I wanted to knock that wall down for her, to take her someplace expensive, le Lion D'or or Tiberios, and treat her to a little luxury.

■ ■ ■ ■

The bank's air conditioner blasted air so cold it gave Mandy goosebumps, but I was sweating while I counted my drawer the next morning, waiting for the right moment to ask Mandy out.

"Maybe we could have dinner together on Saturday," I said softly as Nelva unlocked the front door and let the first customer in. "Someplace downtown ... a French restaurant."

She smiled. "Sorry, Freddy. Can't afford it."

"Leave that to me. I've hardly spent any money this summer."

"How much have you saved?" she asked.

"Over eight hundred dollars," I whispered.

"But you need that money," said Mandy.

"I'd rather spend it on you than on the University of Maryland."

"Spend it on yourself, go to New York. That's what I would do. Not New York, but somewhere."

A woman came to my window to pay her phone bill, and Mandy got busy with a cashier's check. It was payday, a strange day at the bank because we cashed people's paychecks all day long, yet we didn't get one. The money was deposited directly into our accounts, more like an allowance than a salary. Payday also meant staggered lunch hours and a long line of customers. Mandy and I didn't have a chance to talk until the doors had been locked and I was balancing my drawer.

"You still haven't answered me," I said, tallying my coins. Happy had already changed into her 7-Eleven uniform, hurriedly counting her money so she wouldn't be late for her second job.

"About?" asked Mandy, bundling her cash, her drawer seventeen cents over.

"Saturday night. Dinner." I took the one-dollar bills out of my drawer and counted them quickly and rhythmically, the way Dixie had trained me.

Mandy stood so close to me I could feel her breath. It made me shiver. I kept my eyes on my money, but could see her cherry-lacquered nails drumming on the table next to me.

She stopped tapping. "It would be wonderful to have dinner with you at an elegant restaurant," she said.

I lost track of the fives and had to start again. Dixie was getting impatient, waiting for my balance sheet, but I was imagining the soft glow of candlelight illuminating Mandy's face. As I totaled the fives and moved onto the tens, Mandy watched me, the same way I'd been watching her for the past month.

"I'm going to miss you when you leave," she said.

I stopped adding my twenties and looked at her.

"That's weeks away," I said. "Besides, it's not like I'm leaving town. I'm not going to New York yet, remember?"

She didn't say anything. I continued counting my twenties, but something was wrong with my drawer. I was short. A thousand dollars short. A cold sweat started along my hairline, and the chilled air made the sweat feel like icicles.

Mandy counted the money. A thousand dollars short. Dixie counted it. Still a thousand dollars short. Nelva got the same total.

"I'm sure I locked my drawer when I went to lunch," I told Nelva, sitting in her office. "It's never unlocked."

"Even when you turn around to check a signature card or type a money order?" she asked. She seemed calm, but I knew she was upset, because she'd refused one of Big Kenny's calls.

"That only takes a few seconds."

"Someone on the line could easily have grabbed a pack of twenties while your back was turned. Especially during payday pandemonium."

Dixie knocked on the door and stuck her head in.

"He's here," she told Nelva.

Nelva stood up. "A policeman will be in to see you in a minute..."

"Policeman?"

"I'm sorry, Freddy. It's procedure. You wait here in my office, okay?" she said softly, winking as she left. I wondered if she was ever this nice to Big Kenny.

She left the door open so I could see him, a tall man with sunglasses wearing a brownish gray uniform. After talking to Nelva for a few minutes, he stood by one of the counters, and each employee was asked to empty their pockets and purses as they exited. Happy had left for the Slurpee machine before the money was discovered missing, but the others lined up, Charles first, with two packs of cigarettes and a Bic lighter. He waved good-bye to me after passing inspection, the first time he'd ever looked me in the eye.

Mandy was next. Her purse was bright red and very small, barely big enough for the nail file, hairbrush, and wallet she kept inside, a little girl's purse in the policeman's large hands, but Mandy paid no attention to him as he rifled through her bag. She looked at me, snapping her fingers. She stopped by the door to Nelva's office on her way out and blew me a kiss.

Tortoiseshell containers of eyeshadow and rouge poured out of Dixie's purse, along with several kinds of lipstick, lip liner, lip gloss, and various brands of hairspray, aerosol and non. It looked like a cosmetics counter and it made me smile, though she looked about to cry when she said, "You keep that 'Teller of the Month' badge on, you hear?"

The policeman came into the office and shut the door.

"Where's the money, son?" he said in an accent not unlike Nelva's, dropped an octave.

"I don't know. I didn't take it." My voice sounded too loud, like I was lying. I felt as if I'd stolen the money.

He asked me to tell him everything I'd done since arriving at work that morning, jotting notes on a little pad he pulled from his shirt pocket. He smiled when I told him about asking Mandy out, as though ready to dispense fatherly advice. After I finished, he took off his sunglasses and rubbed his eyes, which were too small and too dark for his fat, sunburned face, tiny black buttons glued onto a pumpkin.

"Young man, you have a choice. Either you give me the money, or I book charges."

"No, I don't have a choice," I said, "because I don't have the money. If you book charges, I still won't have the money."

He stood up.

"Do you know a good lawyer, Fred?" he asked.

I thought of my father passed out on the couch, his pants undone, his mouth open.

"No," I answered, "I do not."

■ ■ ■ ■

Mandy called me late that night.

"Did I wake the entire house?" she whispered into the phone.

"A large explosion wouldn't wake my parents," I said. "They're too drunk. And I'm too hot to sleep."

"Crank up the air conditioner," she suggested.

"My father won't let me use it," I said. "He prides himself on keeping the windows open and the air conditioner off no matter how hot the heat wave."

"What did he say about the missing money?" Mandy asked.

"I didn't tell him. He's a lawyer, not a detective."

I told Mandy that Nelva suspected someone on the line.

"Dixie wouldn't jeopardize fourteen years at the bank for a thousand dollars," I said, "and I know you need money, but if you were going to steal, it wouldn't be from me."

"Charles?" said Mandy.

"He doesn't have the guts."

"That leaves Happy."

"She'd left the bank by the time I counted my drawer," I said. "Did she take the pack of twenties with her?"

After we said good night, all I could think of was the theft. I pictured Happy Ho in her brown-and-orange 7-Eleven uniform, standing by a Slurpee machine till midnight, then getting up early the next morning to go work at the bank, her eyes weary, her feet throbbing, her hands reaching into my drawer, and I was still awake when the sun began to rise, casting its harsh morning light across my pillow. I showered and dressed for work an hour early, but the heat made it harder for my father to wake up. It would look bad to be late this morning, so I took his car keys off his dresser and drove myself to work, expecting every police car I passed to pull me over for robbing a bank, or stealing a car, or both.

Dixie was the only one who beat me to the bank.

"Listen, Freddy, you can't handle any money today. Company policy," she told me. "I'll find something for you to do, like organizing signature cards."

I had expected this, taking a box of poorly alphabetized cards and sitting at the desk nearest the front door. Outside, Nelva stepped out of the passenger's side of a pickup truck, giving me a glimpse of why she called him "Big" Kenny as the truck squealed out of the parking lot. I started sorting through the A's, setting aside accounts that had been closed.

Charles's soft voice took me by surprise.

"I thought you could use this," he said, handing me a button that read, "Don't let the turkeys get you down!" He pinned it onto my shirt, below my name tag and the "Teller of the Month" badge, and I waited for Mandy to walk through the door and laugh at my being decorated like a war hero.

But Happy Ho was next.

"Sorry I'm late," she said, rushing into the bank. "The Slurpee machine break down last night and I didn't get home until two a.m." She wondered why I was sitting at the front desk, and when I told her about the missing money, she seemed to know nothing about it.

"Where's Mandy?" she asked. Nelva tried calling Mandy's number, but her phone had been shut off.

"Probably didn't pay her bill," said Dixie, and I wondered where Mandy had called me from the night before.

The bank opened at nine o'clock, two tellers short. I looked at the closed teller windows, side by side, and tried to imagine Mandy stealing from my drawer. At first I couldn't picture it, but as the hours passed and Mandy didn't appear, my disbelief turned into anger. I could see her committing the crime, though my vision of it remained blurry and unfocused, like the film of a bank robbery captured on hidden camera. I wished the movie had a different ending: me turning around and catching her in the act, slamming my drawer shut, and bruising her tapered fingers, breaking a glossy nail.

Everyone on the line wanted Mandy caught, but when the policeman showed up in the late afternoon, he told us Mandy had fled, taking her clothes and leaving behind what little furniture she owned.

"You're out of the hot seat, Fred," he said, smiling at me, his teeth as yellow as Charles's fingernails.

I was also out of a job.

"We have to cash in *your* bond to replace the money, because the only proof against Mandy is circumstantial," Nelva explained, "and if we cash in your bond, we have to fire you. The insurance company insists."

She didn't seem rural when she shook my hand, acting on behalf of the bank. Dixie hugged me, blue mascara running down her cheeks, and Charles gave me a surprisingly firm handshake, his nails digging into my palm. Happy smiled, saying, "You come to 7-Eleven anytime. I give you free Slurpee."

"Forget the Slurpee," I said. "I'll just stop by and visit with you."

Nelva offered to keep my account open, but I closed it, not sure when I'd be ready to step inside the bank without feeling the humiliation of having trusted the wrong person.

"Large bills or small?" asked Dixie, always the pro, counting out $873.46, my total savings for the summer.

I drove along the loop of highway that surrounded the city, again and again passing the exit to my parents' house, the exit to Mandy's, the exit to the University of Maryland, and the big green sign promising, "New York, 250 miles." I wondered if Mandy had turned off there, fleeing as far as she could on one thousand dollars, farther than New York. She'd probably made her escape the night before, as soon as she'd left the bank, stopping at her apartment to throw some clothes into the car. She could have been hundreds of miles away when she called me to find out if her plan was working, if her friendship with me would keep her above suspicion until she didn't show up at the bank.

It was dark when I got home, returning my father's car. I was ready for his drunken wrath, but it wasn't the car he was angry about. My mother gave me a tearful look and left the room as my father started to pace, lips clamped around his cigar.

"Patrick Mulgrew called this evening," he said. "He wanted to say how sorry he was about what happened. Imagine his surprise when he discovered I didn't know. You weren't man enough to tell me yourself?"

"I didn't take the money."

"Mulgrew explained that," my father said evenly. "He told me about that girl, the one who got herself pregnant. The bank takes her back and this is how she repays them..."

"Them?" I said. "It was me she stole from, my drawer she robbed."

"Why didn't you tell me?" asked my father, a lawyer posing the key question.

"What could you have done?" I asked.

"I'm an attorney," he shouted.

"So what could you have done?"

"I'm your father," he said quietly, and I realized he was sober.

I climbed the stairs to my room.

"You're on your own," he yelled after me. "I'm not getting you another job, and you won't get one yourself with this on your record. They've cashed in your bond, mister."

At the top of the stairs I turned and tossed his keys down to him. He caught them, shouting, "You pull that car stunt again and I'll have you arrested. Driving without a license, automobile theft..."

My father was still screaming after I closed my bedroom door.

"You can forget college for this year. You're obviously not mature enough. Just forget University of Maryland."

I already had forgotten it. I took off my name tag, the button Charles gave me, my "Teller of the Month" badge. The sky outside my window was filled with stars, the same stars that shine over New York City, and I realized I'd never know why Mandy stole the money from my drawer. Perhaps she wanted me to close my account, take the money, and run. I pulled the $873.46 out of my pocket and counted it like a bank teller. I didn't know where Mandy had gone, but I knew where I was going.

RED LIGHT

Claire landed in the City with unlimited material but no marketable skills, out of work until Macy's hired her as an elf for Santa's Workshop because she looked the part: short and round. They gave her red tights, a green costume, and pointed shoes, with a feathered hat to hide her long blonde hair. It was the only hat she owned, and she told me she wore it to keep her head warm during the seventy-block walk to her apartment just below Harlem, often unable to afford even a subway token on her elfin salary.

I'd also come to New York to be a comedian, equipped with ten minutes of material and extensive retail experience, having spent my one year out of high school inside a suburban mall. I'd learned where the real money was soon after I arrived, and though I was fired from my first waitering job for ignoring the owner's "No children allowed" edict, I had honed my serving skills at restaurant number two by the time I met Claire, who'd turned in her tights the day after Christmas, again looking for work. My lanky arms were loaded with plates when she came into the restaurant carrying a handbag large enough to contain props, the corner of her oversized purse grazing a customer's cheek as she passed, knocking over the next table's bud vase.

"I'm sorry," she said, not knowing where to aim her apology, then speaking to her bag, "I can't take you anywhere."

Her voice was too loud for the dainty dining room, but Claire's timing was perfect: the former cappuccino girl had stormed out in the middle of the shift, and someone had to make the coffee, so Claire was hired to handle the cappuccino machine and the counter that surrounded it, a row of stools where customers sat if all they wanted was coffee. The machine was bigger than she was, brass and beautiful with levers, knobs, and gauges, and she was put to work with minimal instruction from the manager, Insaf, a Lebanese immigrant whose outfits were pressed, pristine, and always out of season, short-sleeved blouses and cotton skirts not warm enough for a New York winter.

I started calling out the orders — "One cappuccino, two mochaccinos, and three sankaccinos" — and though Claire tried to keep up à la Lucille Ball, her apron was soon stained with espresso, the gleaming machine splattered with steamed milk. Insaf was never without a sponge to wipe up the spills and fight the label of dirty foreigner, but she didn't find Claire's incompetence funny that first night, and Claire was about to be fired when I intervened, charmed by her husky voice and sensing in her the kind of spontaneity that my overly scripted act was missing. My private-school education hadn't prepped me for much, yet it seemed to grant me some sort of clout with the predominantly third-world staff, and Claire was saved. As I was leaving, I heard a high-pitched voice thanking me. I couldn't figure out who was talking until I spotted a tiny chocolate cookie shaped like a man, dancing on the countertop, and the huddled figure of Claire hiding behind the counter, making the cookie move like a marionette. I grabbed a man-shaped sugar cookie and crouched on the other side of the counter, telling Claire's cookie, "You're welcome." Soon our cookies were doing a dance, their baked bodies touching until Claire pressed too hard, snapping my cookie in half.

Claire served no food: I was summoned if her customers wanted to eat. The cappuccino machine was her only responsibility, but it kept her there long after I'd tallied my tips, much more than she made pouring coffee. Sometimes I'd wait while she took the machine apart to clean it, unscrewing and detaching until its parts cluttered her counter, then polishing the brass with milky blue liquid. Afterwards I'd help her put it back together, the two of us giggling over the complicated mechanics of cappuccino while Insaf waited impatiently, unable to leave until we were finished. Usually I'd walk Claire to the subway station, waving as she disappeared down the steps, then heading to a nearby bar, where I'd order a beer so my hands would have something to hold as I looked around the crowded room.

Claire had been at the restaurant for several weeks when I spotted her through the tinted window of the bar, walking up Broadway minutes after we'd said good night at the subway stairs.

"Are the trains down?" I asked, stepping outside and startling her.

"They are," she said, refusing my offer to loan her cab fare. I told her I'd buy her a drink.

"Gay bars aren't good for a girl's morale," said Claire. "Now go back inside and get yourself a man."

I'd gotten one man since moving here, an Andy Warhol wanna-be whose attraction to my youth soon waned, the way a jaded graduate grows bored with a freshman's zeal. Claire felt like a classmate, so I went back inside and got my coat, catching up with her on the next block, touching her shoulder when I got within reach and leaving my hand there as we walked. She was almost a foot shorter than I, her arm around my waist. We were an odd-looking pair, Claire all circles, large breasts and curly hair next to my long lines and sharp angles, and people we passed seemed to notice us. It was early March, the weather still wintry, so we held each other tight, and though it felt good, I expected at some point we'd get on a bus or take a taxi. But when the music from the boom boxes began to grow louder, the lyrics of "Nine to Five" becoming "Nueve a Cinco," I realized we were going to walk all the way to Claire's apartment.

"You're not scared?" I asked.

"I do this every night," she confessed. "I wait at the bottom of the subway steps until you've gone, and then I walk."

"Why?"

"Money," said Claire. "Not everyone's a star waiter with a trust fund."

"The trust-fund part isn't true."

"At least you can pay your rent," she said. "I'm months behind, still working on January."

"I want your landlord," I laughed.

"You wouldn't want my building. No heat, no lights in the hallway, no locks on the front door."

It was as bad as she'd said it would be, the lobby dirty, the stairway dark, but her apartment had a party atmosphere, decorated with streamers, the only touch of color Claire could afford. She'd found a roommate to share expenses, and I assumed it was he who grabbed her bag before she closed and bolted the door, rifling through her purse as though he'd snatched it.

"What'd you bring me?" he asked. His dark hair was slicked back and under control, but his turquoise eyes looked hungry, and I remembered Claire telling me that the first thing he'd said about himself when he answered her ad was "I'm adopted," relaying his sketchy adoption records like they were his only credentials, as if he'd just come from the orphanage and not his middle-class home in South Jersey, moving back to the city of his birth in search of his natural mother.

From inside her handbag he lifted two slices of cheesecake, which I recognized from the restaurant. Claire set up some pillows to serve as a sofa as the roommate opened a bottle of champagne, the cork bouncing off a bare wall.

"A gift from a man," he told me, skillfully filling my mug.

"Nice man," I said.

"One of many," said the roommate.

"And they all come bearing gifts," said Claire. "My men just come, then go."

"Love 'em and leave 'em?" I asked.

"Without the love," she said.

"My boyfriends love you," said the roommate, strumming a guitar. His bright smile suggested show tunes, but the song he started singing was his own, in a voice more whiskey than champagne. The roommate's song was simple, immediately familiar the way good folk songs are, and by the second verse I knew the words to the refrain. Usually I was self-conscious about my singing, but I was on my second mug of champagne and Claire had joined in, her husky voice hard-core yet honey-coated. I barely realized I was singing along until the roommate stopped playing, laughing too hard to continue.

"What's so funny?" asked Claire.

"You two, singing together," he explained, still laughing. "It's like Julie Andrews and Janis Joplin, together at last."

We started to sing again, Claire shoveling more gravel into her voice and me adding a British accent. Soon I was Julie Andrews crooning "Me and Bobby McGee" while Claire did Joplin's version of "I Could Have Danced All Night." When he wasn't accompanying us on the guitar, her roommate became the audience for us to patter with, telling tales of *Mary Poppins* and *Monterey Pop*, and by the time they walked me down the four flights of stairs to wait with me on their dangerous street until a cab came by, the sun was starting to rise.

Julie and Janis became a popular pair with the restaurant staff. Even Insaf was delighted by our duets, though she was too recent an immigrant to understand what we were spoofing, laughing at the sheer contrast between Claire's gritty voice and my private-school tones. A few of Claire's regulars were also in on our act, though Claire hardly needed my help to entertain them, making her customers laugh so hard it seemed their coffee was spiked. The restaurant had no liquor license, but Claire ran her counter like a bar, slapping down demitasse as if they were shot glasses, topping a cappuccino with a cloud of foam, like beer on tap. It was Claire's stage, though I was sometimes called over as guest star, the whole room watching as I stepped behind her bar for what were becoming our bits.

For the first time, I felt funny in New York. I'd already auditioned my set at several clubs, waiting all day with other would-be comedians to secure a good spot but still going on at two a.m., doing the full ten minutes whether there were five people or fifty in the audience, determined to pay my dues. So far, the only person I'd really made laugh was my landlord, by listing "standup comic" as my occupation on an apartment application.

"You're too tall, too blond, too handsome," he told me. "You don't look funny."

"But I am," I said seriously. "I'm very funny."

He didn't require proof, just my father's co-signature on the lease, the one time I'd called home for help. The crowds in the comedy rooms were harder to please, and though Claire talked a lot about "when I start playing the circuit," she'd yet to take her act outside the restaurant and into a club, not ready to try her material without a counter to lean on.

"I can't make comedy without making cappuccino," she said. "I'm only funny while foaming milk."

"You could lug the machine to an open-mike night," I suggested, "and serve coffee as you do your set."

Which is how Claire got her first booking: serving coffee. It was a tip from a customer, a dollar bill wrapped around a business card with a date and a time scribbled on it. She was to do twenty minutes at an East Side club known for a red light that flashed on when acts weren't funny, cutting the comedian short. I'd never played there, afraid that getting a red light would put a halt to my hopes for success. I could do my entire set in silence by blaming the audience for having no sense of humor, and though the red light was obviously controlled by a person in a booth, it seemed omniscient, the final word on talent, and I wasn't sure what it would say about mine.

Claire didn't seem frightened.

"It's my big break," she said, buffing the brass.

"Twenty minutes is a long time," I told her, knowing that ten minutes seemed endless when no one was laughing.

"I do eight hours here."

"With a little help."

"With a lot of help." She smiled. "So why don't we celebrate? Break open champagne, make scrambled eggs, even take a taxi."

I told her I was too tired, leaving her to assemble the machine on her own. My apartment wasn't air-conditioned, already hot in May, and I sat in the dark thinking of my act: jokes about being teased in junior high ("Not just students, teachers too"), one-liners about losing weight ("If the Beverly Hills diet didn't work for you, try the Beverly Hillbillies': unlimited portions of Granny's victuals washed down with Texas tea"). I'd written it in my parents' house, and though they hadn't read it, my father's secretary had, telling me she'd laughed out loud while typing the final version, though I'd since realized that years of looking at legal documents had left her easily entertained. I felt embarrassed by my act's mediocrity, and also angry at Claire, for I'd done things the right way, paying my rent on time and writing my jokes down, and she ended up with the booking. I fell asleep on my sofa, the fold-out mattress folded in. I was still wearing a waiter's uniform, my pocket bulging with single dollar bills.

The phone rang around dawn, though in my drowsiness I wasn't sure if the sun was rising or setting. For a moment I thought I'd slept through the next day, expecting to hear Insaf's voice when I answered, asking me where I was. Instead, I heard loud music and someone laughing, and when she spoke I knew it was Claire, obviously at a pay phone and obviously drunk.

"You're easier to carry than a cappuccino machine," she said.

"What are you talking about?" I asked. "Where are you?"

"I'm not sure where I am, but I know what I'm talking about," she told me. "We're going to be partners."

"In crime?"

"In comedy. I hate being alone offstage. Why would I want be alone onstage?"

Her dime was up and she had no more money, which meant another long walk from wherever she was. I offered to pick her up in a cab, but we were cut off, and though I was concerned for Claire's safety, I soon fell back asleep, Claire doing stand-up in my dreams, alone on a huge stage surrounded by flashing red lights.

■ ■ ■ ■

My living room set and stereo unit reminded Claire of Macy's, since Santa's workshop shared a floor with the furniture department, so we met at her apartment. I arrived for our first rehearsal expecting to find Claire still sleeping, but she answered her door on the first ring, wrapped in a kimono and ready to work. She'd bought me a mug with my name on it ("in lieu of a director's chair," she said), a notebook, and a box of crayons. Coffee was made ("by a pro," she reminded me), and I couldn't believe this was the same Claire who showed up late for work almost every night, lying to Insaf about a broken-down bus or stuck subway car, then telling me about the previous night's escapade, the same story (a bar, a man, a hangover that made her oversleep for the five p.m. shift) with different details.

"I met him at a lesbian bar where I can always find free drinks and asked, 'What's a guy like you doing in a place like this?'" or "I felt like Louis Armstrong playing the flute," or even raunchier, "I couldn't remember where I'd left my diaphragm until it turned up in the most obvious place."

She was serious about her comedy, and we rehearsed daily except Sunday, when both of us worked brunch at the restaurant. We had four weeks to write our act, passing the notebook back and forth like a Ouija board, my perfect penmanship becoming her childish scrawl, sometimes in midword. We started with the cookies, as we had the night we met, turning our first fumbled exchange into *Food Is Talking*, a TV show exploring the tension between vanilla and chocolate.

Our entire set was based on contrasts: male-female, tall-short, skinny-plump, but what bonded us together during the long days at her apartment and even longer nights at work was the similarity of our situations: same age, same goal, same restaurant. It was like falling in love, an experience neither of us had known, and often the first thing I'd do after getting home from one of our fourteen-hour days was call Claire and talk for two more. She'd tell me about driving cross-country with her mother, Dolores, who'd left a trail of unpaid motel bills, drunk-driving tickets, and husband Cubby back in Boston. California wasn't far enough, so Dolores took six-year-old Claire on her first plane trip to Hawaii, where the two of them lived on Claire's child support. Dolores died after a decade of bourbon, sending Claire back to the mainland and her father's new family. She'd been there a month when ex-smoker Cubby was diagnosed with lung cancer, leaving what little there was to the second wife, except a ten-thousand-dollar life insurance policy that Claire squandered in a year, buying expensive clothes for herself and expensive equipment for a local band whose bass player Claire had a crush on.

Claire had saved few souvenirs from her exotic past: some pictures of her younger self surrounded by tropical flowers, and a ukulele that had no strings when she first showed it to me, playing air guitar like a Hawaiian Hendrix, the ukulele looking as undersized and out of proportion as the tiny talk-show set we'd built for the cookies. We didn't know how it fit in, but we knew it was funny, so her roommate, who in the process of trying to locate his mother had learned Where to Find It Buy It Eat It in New York, directed us to a midtown block with music supply stores lining either side of the street. Claire chose one because its window displayed the same state-of-the-art bass she'd bought her beloved guitarist.

"Aloha," Claire said to the man inside as he stretched four strings over the ukulele, "we're doing a musical version of *Hawaii Five-O.*"

He didn't laugh, carefully tuning the ukulele with a pitchfork for perfect sound, and we met many such men on many such blocks while outfitting our act. We found the fake-flower district, the street specializing in sequins, a store that sold only feathers, where we spent an afternoon sorting through piles of plumage for the costume Claire was making, Claire pulling what she wanted and me paying the bill, five dollars for a shopping bag full of feathers, pink and white. The bag felt empty when the salesclerk handed it to me, but as Claire and I walked the two miles to work, it seemed to fill with possibilities, and I felt about the feathers like a child who cherishes a found bauble, believing its magic powers will protect him from all of life's red lights.

I don't know what protected Claire during her late-night walks and one-night stands before I became her rescue squad, answering my phone on the first ring no matter how sound my sleep, how vivid my dream. I'd write down the address, barely able to understand her slurred speech, though often it wasn't Claire speaking, and I'd know she'd drunkenly dialed my number, passed the phone to another person, and passed out. I lived on the outskirts of Claire's dangerous life, and I thrilled to the adventure of it, telling the taxi driver a street I'd never heard of in a neighborhood I didn't know, then speeding through the night down the City's deserted streets, running red lights and making illegal turns. Once Claire called me collect from New Jersey and I had to meet her bus at the station to pay her fare, but the farthest I ever traveled to get her was Coney Island, and I remember seeing the sun rise over the Brooklyn Bridge as my cab crossed the East River, its meter continually clicking, the fare already greater than I'd ever paid. This was a view of New York I wouldn't have had without Claire, and in those minutes just after dawn the City looked gentle and harmless, like a hardened criminal might in his sleep, and I was safe in my knowledge of how much Claire needed me.

She never called her roommate, though he was usually awake when I pulled Claire out of the cab and sometimes carried her upstairs, stopping on each landing to reposition, holding her over my narrow shoulder or cradling her heft in my arms and using my foot to knock on the door. Her roommate always seemed irritated by the interruption, barely saying hello before he resumed studying his photocopies of 1950s social registers for records of the more riotous coming-out balls, convinced he was the folly of a fallen debutante. Had he gone as far back as the forties he might have found my father, only child of a prominent family, first in his class and star of his school plays. Claire had talent on both sides, Dolores a former dancer who'd still looked good doing a drunken hula in Hawaii, and Cubby the campus clown with rave reviews from his college paper, which Claire read aloud as if he'd been on Broadway. My father's clippings covered the walls of the house I grew up in, laminated articles praising his legal mind, for he'd left theatre behind in law school.

No wall space was left in my father's den for my achievements, though so far the only thing I had that was suitable for framing was the flyer for our show. We couldn't afford photos ("Yet," Claire stressed) so she drew a cartoon of the two of us wearing leis, billing our act as "A Luau of Laughter!" We had no mailing list, distributing our flyer by hand to every specialty store we'd shopped at, and though it hardly fit the decor of our restaurant, Insaf let us paper the front door with our little pink postcards. The cappuccino machine was surrounded by them, and when Insaf wasn't listening, Claire would promise her counter customers a free cappuccino for those who came to our act, the same way she'd load her large purse with sugar packets and flatware when Insaf's head was turned.

We didn't have to steal the *Food Is Talking* cookies: Insaf gave them to us, an unexpected contribution, for Insaf was a rigid woman who did not believe in the exception to the rule. Initially she'd even been reluctant to promise us the night off, but as the gig got closer, she used her immigrant skills at adapting to new worlds to develop a sort of show-business savvy, wishing us, "Break your legs," in broken English, and asking us about the size of the house, the size of our cut. These were questions Claire wanted answered, but she was afraid to talk to the man who'd booked her, afraid he'd take away his generous tip. I was too, though I'd listened to my father's phone conversations enough to fake a lawyerly lingo, so I agreed to arrive at the club before Claire and map out the details.

I got there so early, the owner wasn't in.

"When is he expected?" I asked one of the less haggard waitresses. She answered with a shrug, not looking at me as she draped red-checkered cloths over the tiny tables. It struck me as an odd staff for a comedy club, since none of them looked capable of laughter, except the bartender, a burly man who laughed out loud when I pulled the leis out of our sequin-studded prop box, ready to give me the red light before the show had started. He was slightly more responsive than the waitress when I asked permission to step onto the stage, and I took his "Whatever" to mean yes.

The first thing I saw was the red light hanging dark and dormant, a caged bulb in the back of the room. I'd expected something hi-tech, but this looked like an ordinary work light, benign as a baseball bat is until the wrong hands get hold of it. Someone in the booth was checking the lights, the stage awash in blue, then yellow, then a spotlight so white it seemed silver. I unloaded our props, hurriedly hiding Claire's ukulele behind a flat, stashing the cookies in the piano, trying to set up before the red light was tested, but it remained unilluminated, ominous even behind its bars.

I sat on a stool with the leis in my lap, watching the bar fill up with comedians who knew the bartender, the waitresses, each other. I'd seen some of them around at the clubs, all men much older than I, and I hoped they didn't remember my solo act, though I was wearing the same costume, a white dinner jacket that had once fit my father, the only blazer I owned. It was too dressy for the smoky club, but I felt half-naked without Claire, unable to perform until the rest of my costume arrived. I'd given Claire money for a taxi, making her promise not to walk, and when I spoke to the owner, who smelled like dry-cleaning fluid and wore a taupe-colored toupee, I asked for cab fare plus five dollars above his initial offer of twenty. He knocked the deal down to a final offer of fifteen, "take it or leave it," and I took it.

Soon the audience came, customers from my restaurant passing me by, not recognizing me without an apron and black pants, but Claire still hadn't arrived when the emcee started the show. I stepped outside to call her from a pay phone on the corner. There was no answer, so I waited in the club, standing by the door, unable to see the stage or the red light, though I knew when it went on by the laughter of the crowd and the sputtering patter of the comedian, like an airplane engine stalled in midflight, the red light burning as the comic crashed, telling the audience how great they'd been even if they'd sat silently through the set. Claire and I had rehearsed our closing comments with no Plan B, no red-light provision, though I'd was more panicked about the opening, for it was minutes away and still no Claire. The emcee warned me that we were on deck, so I had to leave my post at the entrance and wait by the side of the stage, my eyes fixed on the front door as I tried to remember lines from my solo set in case Claire didn't show.

I felt like a bridegroom left at the altar, my blazer adorned with a red boutonniere for our debut, but when she finally rushed through the front door, Claire hardly looked like anyone's bride. She'd wanted to surprise me with her costume, and it shocked the people she passed as she raced by the bar to the performers' holding pen, her clear-plastic dress clinging to her body like cellophane, revealing a hot pink bra and Hawaiian-print panties. Her short hemline was trimmed with the feathers we'd bought, and there were feathers in her hair, which was frizzed out and teased up, leaving her large face exposed and heavily made-up, her eyelids the color of purple orchids and her lips a startling red. It was the face she wore on her late-night binges, though I'd never seen it sober until now, and I realized what an amazing face Claire had, for no amount of makeup could hide the elf that Macy's had hired.

There was barely time to toss a lei around her neck. We'd written an intro for the emcee, but he did his own, something mean about me being prettier but Claire having bigger tits. I'd also asked for a blackout, which we got, the two of us disappearing behind a flat so the stage was empty when the lights came up. First I peeked my head out, singing the opening line of a Polynesian folk song, then Claire popped her head out above mine, as though she were taller, the crowd laughing before she'd sung, even more when they heard her husky voice. And now our entrance, stepping into full view and reversing our height difference, me towering over Claire as she strummed her ukulele. I could see our reflection in the back mirror: a 1940s movie star and a tropical bird moving toward the audience, riding a wave of laughter that rolled through the room, reaching its peak as we reached the edge of the stage. It felt as if we were surfing, shifting our weight to stay on top of the laughter, leaping high into the air and landing back on our board, exhilarated but in control. During the bigger laughs I watched the crowd, Claire's roommate sitting alone at a side table, in between men and still with no mother. Her regular customers were clustered near the back, and through it all, the interracial cookie bit, the Janis Joplin–Julie Andrews jam session, the red light watched us from its cage, the audience laughing loud enough to keep the light off long after we'd used up our time and spilled into the next comic's slot.

■ ■ ■ ■

Insaf viewed our success as a scheduling nightmare, for out of that first booking came a standing Saturday-night gig. She begrudgingly shuffled some shifts to give us Saturdays off, making it clear that no more props would be provided by the restaurant.

"You must pay full price," she said.

"Talk to Freddy," Claire told her. "He's the money man."

I was in charge of how we spent money because it was my money we were spending. Claire asked me to keep a tally of our expenses, promising to pay me back her share of the props, the flyers, the taxis and dinners. She offered to give me her portion of our pay, but I was only able to get the club owner back up to twenty, and Claire needed the ten dollars, which would have barely made a dent in her debt. Talking about money made both of us tense: I'd grown up with plenty of it, never worrying about money until my father cut me off for choosing comedy over college. And though Claire was young to have regrets, she had a big one about the spree she'd had with her inheritance, a genie's wish foolishly wasted.

Our financial discussions were short and dry, nothing funny about them, but we never fought about money the way she did with her roommate, who wanted her half of the rent on the first of every month. He'd taken over the larger room because of her late payments, banishing Claire to the back bedroom, too small for us to rehearse in. There was room to work in my apartment, and though Claire found it sterile ("Another word for clean?" I asked), she was glad to get away from her roommate's stacks of birth certificates, his constant phone calls to women who might be his mother, for he had a new lead that looked legitimate, and he now referred to the woman who'd raised him as Aunt Peggy, saving Mom for his rich and rightful mother.

Less work got done at my apartment: the urgency that had fueled our early rehearsals was diffused, since we had thirty minutes of proven material to carry us through our upcoming appearances. Claire called every morning to say she was running late, and we'd usually start with a long lunch at a nearby diner, mining material for new ideas: "a suburban housewife who's appointed pope and covers all pews in plastic" or "an urban girl who can't get a date without her Fairy Godfather," and a starring role for me as manager of a midwestern McDonald's who's transferred to a midtown Manhattan branch, hawking "Happy Meals" and Ronald McDonald buttons to hustlers and heroin addicts. But my apartment lacked the desperate atmosphere of Claire's. It wasn't a place you'd do anything to get out of, so instead of writing we'd talk, more about the future than the past, dreaming of Johnny Carson and later, our own TV special. The club was billing us as "The Next Nichols and May," but we wanted to be bigger, and though I saw our path as an expressway with no speed limit, Claire seemed more aware of the distance we'd have to travel.

"If you drive to Florida," she told me, "you're not surprised when you get there."

She wasn't getting anywhere at work, still stuck behind the counter. Several waitresses had been hired recently, and Claire resented being passed over for prettier girls, chained to the cappuccino machine, unable to make good money.

"You're too messy," said Insaf when Claire asked for a chance on the floor, and though Claire tried to clean up her act, her machine gleaming after the busiest of rushes, she remained stuck behind her counter, refusing to speak to the new waitresses while filling their coffee orders. Sometimes she barely spoke to me, as though I roamed the length of the restaurant merely to rub in how trapped she was, though she knew I pleaded her case whenever there was an opening, only to get Insaf's same verdict, "Too messy."

Messy is what had made her regular customers laugh, and the more she tried to prove her worth as a waitress, the less funny she was at work, saving her comedy for the club. No more bits were born behind her counter, but onstage she took off, and if we'd been surfing that first night, Claire was now soaring like a rocket, fire shooting from her engines and burning me as badly as the red light when my timing was off, which hers never was. Claire could conquer the slowest of crowds, softening the punchlines and stopping at the first laugh, no matter how lame, to nod in smiling approval of the audience's hip sense of humor, as if they were performing for her. Sometimes I felt I was performing for her also, gauging my ability by her response rather than the audiences', feeling like a failure when Claire didn't laugh.

Usually the crowd had big laughs for both of us, and though I figured she was the favorite, I no longer felt I was lying when I called myself a comedian. A few people in the club had seen me do stand-up, but their recollections were vague, so my solo act was soon forgotten, and though I never showed Claire my ten-minute set, she made barbed comments about it, the way a second wife loathes the first without ever having met her.

It was like being married, the passion of sex replaced by performing, and at the club, we were a couple both on- and offstage, clinging to each other in the holding pen where everyone else was heterosexual and male, their material made up of fag cracks and tit jokes, with a bit of bathroom humor to get the bartender laughing. The only act that made Claire and me laugh was the Triple "A," a trio of comedians named Alan who moved "The Three Little Pigs" into New York apartments and turned the wicked wolf into a landlord attempting to evict them. The Alans were booked sporadically by the owner, but Claire and I were part of the club's core of comics, granting us immunity from the red light. I'd watched it happen to many comedians, the only time the wooden-faced waitresses laughed. Some nights it lit up during a solid set and let others drag on in silence, but no matter how terrible the material, there was a moment of shock, the way a police siren causes panic even when it's not you they're pulling over. This light didn't flash, an unblinking blaze of fiery red sounding a silent alarm that would've sent me running from the club as far as I could, farther than my apartment, maybe back to my parents' house.

Most of those who got the light fled to the bar, buying a drink from the bartender who'd just booed them, dissecting their set to see what went wrong. Often Claire would console them, and though she knew where the flaws in their material were, she shared her diagnosis only with me, nursing the comic's wounded ego rather than doctoring his act, playing comedy's Florence Nightingale in exchange for free drinks. She always stayed sober until our set was over, waiting for the next red light to flatter the comedian who'd been cut short. Soon they'd be sitting together at the bar doing shots of bourbon, and though sometimes I'd have a beer to wind down, I had to wake up early for work so I never stayed long after locking our prop box in the owner's office and divvying up our fee. Claire also worked Sunday brunch, but I knew she'd be late the next morning, no longer bothering with excuses for Insaf. One week she didn't show up at all, calling in sick and, with no sleep, probably sounding it.

Now that I was a part of Claire's nightlife, I actually knew less about it. I assumed she went home with whoever bought her the most drinks, and I could tell by the way the comedians looked at her that she'd become the consolation prize for red-light victims, merchandise given to losers on a game show. But I no longer got lurid details and late-night phone calls, and though I welcomed my uninterrupted sleep, I worried about her walking through the City by herself, and wondered who she was turning to for help. Perhaps her roommate had become her rescuer, for his new name had made him a new person. He was now Donny, the name he'd been given at birth by his natural mother. They'd been reunited by telephone: she didn't live on the East Side, or even the East Coast, but in Lincoln, Nebraska, where she'd moved from Brooklyn months after giving him up for adoption. She'd since had two husbands and a legitimate daughter named Darlene, a few years younger than Donny, and though she cried tears of joy during their long-distance calls, she was not what he'd had in mind, a midwestern waitress named Wanda Gail.

He didn't call her Mom, but he called himself Donny, which Claire said was killing the couple who'd adopted him. It was hard to get used to his new name, and when he called my apartment looking for Claire one afternoon, it took me a moment to remember who Donny was.

"Claire's roommate," he reminded me without mentioning his former name. "Is she there?"

I handed her the phone. She was lying on the sofa, her eyes closed, exhausted not from the previous night but from that afternoon's rehearsal, for we'd been unable to come up with new bits that worked, and after three months, the club owner was growing tired of our material. Whatever Donny said woke her up, and she sat at the edge of the couch uttering one-word questions.

"Today?" she gasped. "Which? And?"

She was looking at me as she spoke, and I couldn't tell if it was good news or bad, waiting for her to hang up, which she did without a good-bye.

"The club just called," she said. "We're reviewed in the *Post.*"

"Is it good?" I asked.

"Donny wasn't sure," she told me, heading for the door, "but we'll know soon enough."

We rushed to the nearest newsstand, Claire grabbing the top copy and flipping through the pages, unfamiliar with the paper's format. She was excited, but I had visions of a review that praised her and panned me, wondering why the club had called her apartment when it was I who handled our business. By the time Claire spotted the headline, "Gotham Gets Another Dynamic Duo!," I felt more relieved than happy, for the review was entirely good, not much more than a blurb saying we struck a funny balance between my "controlled restraint" and her "zany antics and throaty voice, which suggests a limitless ability to make people laugh."

"That's us," Claire told the Pakistani man who sold us the paper, holding it open to our page, and then to a woman buying a fashion magazine, "We're the dynamic duo."

Insaf had already seen the review when we got to work, and though she'd taped a copy next to the cappuccino machine, she seemed almost saddened by it, as if our next step would take us out of the restaurant. Some of Claire's customers came by to congratulate us, shaking my hand and hugging her, special-requesting their favorite bits, but we were both too busy. Insaf watched from the counter, helping Claire with the cappuccinos, making sure the dynamic duo did their job, not their act, and by the time Insaf locked the front door, I'd made enough money for an expensive midnight meal.

"We'll have a feast," I told Claire as she shined the machine. "Anywhere you want."

"I can't," she said, her back turned toward me, her face reflected in the brass, blurred and gilded. "Donny's making me dinner."

We walked to the subway in silence, like newlyweds after the reception, drained from the excitement of the day and the pressure of being partners for life with a person you hardly know. I gave her money for the fare and continued walking past my apartment and into the night, stopping at newsstands along the way and staring at the stack of papers. Sometimes I'd buy one, pulling from the middle of the pile as if to make sure my name appeared in every copy, and when I finally stepped inside a bar downtown, my white waiter's shirt was smudged with ink.

I hadn't been to a gay bar since Claire and I formed the act, and either the faces had changed or mine had, because no one used to notice me much and now men were looking. I ordered a beer, averting the gazes of guys I wasn't attracted to until I spotted hair of Hollywood silver framing a young man's face.

"What's your name?" he asked.

I said nothing, drying the bar with a cocktail napkin before opening the paper to page 36 and pointing. For a moment he wasn't sure where to look, following my eyes to my finger and reading the review aloud, slowly and clearly, like an anchorman. I listened, imagining the words enlarged and laminated and hanging in my father's den, but the large print made it easier to read between the lines, and the only name I saw there was Claire's.

It was my name this man was interested in, and I liked the way he broadcast it throughout the bar, later whispering it in my ear, asking me to go home with him. I pictured myself calling Claire, waking her in the middle of the night or maybe interrupting her dinner with Donny, and I wondered if she'd come get me. Again the man said my name, his tongue touching my ear and making me shiver, but I knew from Claire's one-night stands that I'd never see him again if I said yes, so I went home alone, leaving the review on the bar, my name circled, my phone number next to it.

■ ■ ■ ■

Our blurb had been blown up to a poster that hung outside the club, so the audience knew they were going to see something funny, their laughter starting as soon as the emcee introduced us. The review brought in new business, and I'd hoped it would bring the man from the bar, but when I scanned the packed room from the stage, I saw every hair color except white. I hadn't mentioned meeting a man to Claire, yet she seemed to sense my disappointment, treating me gently onstage, letting my laughs go on longer than usual before bulldozing over me. Afterwards she got very drunk on the champagne the club owner served to celebrate our success, raising our fee to forty, top dollar for an act with no TV exposure. Even the waitresses seemed happy for us, and the bartender was pouring whatever we wanted. I closed the club with Claire, staying long after last call, the Triple "A" doing their *Tonight Show* bit (Johnny, Ed, and Doc), Claire and me the guests. Claire's hands brushed hair out of Johnny's face, rested on Ed's thigh, played with Doc's lapels, and though it was obvious she wanted to get in a cab with one, two or all three of the Alans, she ended up with me, the taxi pulling over for her to get sick.

By the time we turned onto her street, her head was in my lap, her eyes closed, so she couldn't see the police car outside her building, its light casting flashes of red inside her lobby. I paid the fare and roused Claire, helping her out of the cab, but it wasn't until a policeman opened the door for us that I saw Donny, sitting on the steps, his face bloodied, one of his eyes swollen shut.

"I'd gone to the bodega for some cigarettes," he was saying as another policeman took notes. "Two black kids jumped me here in the lobby."

"You shouldn't have been out at this hour," said the cop. "You could've been killed."

"They only got two bucks," Donny told him.

"They'll knife you for one."

The policeman with the notepad read back Donny's description of the kids, his phone number, his name, which, even dazed and traumatized, he'd given as Donny. The other cop took my name and number, staring at Claire's see-through dress as if he were going to ticket her for indecent exposure. They offered to drive Donny to the hospital, but he didn't want to go, so I helped him up the stairs, leaving Claire in the lobby with only the banister to lean on. Donny and I had reached his door before I realized that his bleeding face was ruining my father's former jacket. I reached in Donny's pocket, feeling the hardness of his thigh as I searched for his keys.

Claire was crying when she finally appeared, having pulled herself up to the fourth floor. Her mascara was running, so both she and Donny had black eyes, and though I assumed her tears were for him, she stumbled past the bathroom where I was cleaning his cuts and collapsed on her bed, still wearing her smeared stage makeup. I turned out her light, but Donny wanted his left on.

"Stay," he said, "until I fall asleep."

I knew what Donny wanted: someone's presence in his room, someone's weight on his mattress, and though I was tempted to touch him, my desire wasn't sexual. I imagined stroking his cheek, brushing his dark hair away from his injured eye, but with his bruises, the slightest caress could have caused him pain, so I sat on the far edge of his bed, looking at the picture on his night table. I knew it was Wanda by the waitress outfit and the blue eyes, standing with Darlene outside their trailer home, holding a sign that read, "Welcome back Donny," as if he were a runaway who'd finally returned. Next to the picture I noticed Claire's notebook, opened to a page covered in red-crayoned writing, which I assumed were ideas for new bits until I spotted three large words printed in the middle, "LOSE THE PARTNER." Claire was snoring from the other room, and I could tell by Donny's breathing that he was asleep, but my own breath had stopped. I closed my eyes and could still see the words, and when I opened them again Claire's writing looked even larger. The ticking of Donny's clock seemed to slow down, each second sounding a low, elongated chime as my heart beat so loudly I was sure it would wake Donny and Claire.

I waited for my heart to quiet down and his clock to speed up before I reached for the notebook and read what were obviously fragments of a phone conversation, I guessed between Claire and the club owner since his name was scribbled repeatedly. Those three words appeared only once, but there were similar suggestions: "Go on your own," "You're the act," "He'll hold you back." It looked like a reporter's notes, neutral and accurate, and nowhere did she record her reaction. I put the book back beside Wanda and Darlene, and wondered what Claire's response had been.

I was late for work the next day, the first time ever, but when I told Insaf about taking care of Donny, she forgave both me and Claire, who hadn't shown up yet.

"Mugged in his own building," she said, with a blend of horror and pride New Yorkers have about how hard it is to live in the City. Claire came halfway through the shift, making herself a strong cappuccino before she could make one for anyone else. Even then she was slow, serving her customers the wrong kind of coffee, brewing espresso filled with grinds. Her usually expressive face looked pained and pinched, and I could tell her head was pounding so I didn't say much to her. Neither did Insaf, until Claire was leaving, stopping Claire at the front door.

"Let me see your bag, please," said Insaf, and I figured she must have seen Claire stashing something inside of it.

"What?" asked Claire.

"Your bag," Insaf repeated.

"This isn't a police state," Claire told her, and then to me, "Gee, Toto, I have a feeling we're not in Lebanon anymore."

Insaf could not be dissuaded, and I didn't know what she'd pull out as she reached into Claire's purse, brownies or mugs or maybe a salt shaker, but when her hands reappeared holding two rolls of toilet paper, both Claire and I laughed. Insaf didn't, searching her bag for other stolen goods. All she could come up with was the toilet tissue, but that was enough to get Claire fired.

I lent her money to get through a week of job hunting, and we tried to speak every night about that day's progress, though it was difficult with Donny around, because Claire was scared to tell him she'd been fired. I agreed to field calls from him, both at the restaurant and my apartment, where Donny thought she spent her days rehearsing, but he never called, not even to thank me for tending his wounds. Neither did the man I'd met at the bar. Still,

I stayed by the phone, staring at my copies of last week's *Post*. I'd meant to send the review to my parents, but the paper already seemed old and yellowed and much too fragile to frame.

Claire didn't come by the restaurant until she had to pick up her final paycheck. Five days had passed since we'd seen each other, our longest separation, and she looked different to me, her wild hair tamed, her makeup muted. She was wearing an "I'm looking for a job" outfit I didn't know she had, red turtleneck and plaid wool skirt, accessorized with an oversized safety pin, not the large earrings and brooches she usually wore.

"The only thing left of my father's money," she said about her clothes. She seemed angry at me for asking, but with Insaf she was contrite.

"All I took was toilet paper," Claire said when Insaf handed her the check. I thought of paper towels and cloth napkins, dinner plates and dessert cups, and I felt a sense of triumph, or perhaps mere safety, that Claire had been fired for doing something wrong, that Insaf suspected what Claire had gotten away with before she'd gotten caught. Claire had a pleading look on her face, but it was my secret wish that was granted by Insaf's refusal to rehire her. Nor would Insaf override restaurant policy and cash Claire's check, leaving her with no money for the weekend. Claire slammed the front door as she left, and I followed her outside, where suddenly it was autumn.

"Take some money," I told her, reaching into the pocket of my apron.

"No." She stopped me. "I've taken too much from you already."

"You have not," I started, but she shook her head in a way that seemed firm and final.

"You'll get twenty for tomorrow night's gig," I said. It was meant as a reminder, but it came out like a question.

"I canceled tomorrow night," she snapped, "indefinitely." Then softly, "We'll set up a new rehearsal schedule as soon as I get a job."

I didn't believe her; I'm not sure she expected me to. I'd watched her soften the glare of the light for other comedians, but I could see it written in red crayon all over her face, "LOSE THE PARTNER" in large letters.

Our hugs were always quick and uncomfortable, Claire lifted off the ground and me stooped over.

"What about the props?" I asked, before letting her go.

"You hold onto them," she said, granting me custody of the sequins and feathers. She crossed the street and started her long walk to other restaurants in other parts of the City.

"Claire," I called after her, "don't you want your ukulele?"

I called her name again, but she'd gone too far, though maybe she realized what she was leaving behind, the way Wanda had left Donny to get where she was going. A brisk breeze blew through my waiter's uniform, and I thought of my father, of the red lights that led him to law school, wondering what I would use as a costume now that the blazer he'd given me was stained with blood. I could still see Claire, and though I knew how little cash she had in her large purse, I didn't fear for her future, watching her walk away from me wearing the warm clothes her father had paid for.

The Clutch

When Andy Warhol died, I thought of Sam, my first friend in the City, before Claire, and then after. He was directing the *Andy Warhol TV Show* when I met him, a monthly hour of interviews that was shown only in Andy's office and Sam's bedroom. Never on TV. Not that I could find, no matter how thoroughly I searched the *TV Guide*.

I saw the show in Sam's bedroom. That's where I usually saw Sam. It was hardly a room, just a bed built into the wall on three sides, leaving one end open to get in and out. There was a window on one of those walls surrounding the bed, but I could never see through it: it had been covered with a canvas screen long before I met Sam. The room was colorless, white walls and white sheets, except for a bright red phone attached to the wall at the foot of the bed. My legs were longer than Sam's, and I would sometimes knock the phone off the hook while we were making love. We would be interrupted by a loud tone and we would laugh, one of the few jokes we shared.

The first night I spent there we slept upside down, our heads below the phone and our feet on the pillows. I had just moved to New York to be a comedian. At least that's what I told everyone: "I'm moving to New York to be a comedian," though I was more interested in the New York part than in comedy. I'd been out of high school for a year, doing a brief stint at a bank before working at the Bloomingdale's in a local mall that was full of New York style yet stuck in the Maryland suburbs. Working at Bloomingdale's was as close to Manhattan as most people I knew ever got, but it wasn't close enough for me, so on a sunny September morning, I rented a U-Haul and said good-bye to my parents. They stood in the driveway, still in their bathrobes, waving with their breakfast napkins, and I was about to pull away when I realized I had no map, no directions.

I rolled down the window.

"How do I get to New York?" I asked.

"Just take a left at the A&P and follow the signs," my mother answered, making it sound simple.

It seemed simple. I had a place to stay until I found an apartment, sleeping on the sofa of a girl whose brother worked with me at Bloomingdale's. I'd even arranged for a transfer to the New York store, where I would be selling chutney at the gourmet food counter. I wasn't sure what chutney was, but I knew I could sell it.

I turned left at the A&P and found the signs my mother had promised, over the Delaware Bridge, along the New Jersey Turnpike. Even after I arrived in the City, every shop window showed signs that I had headed in the right direction. A pair of heavy clogs, in which I looked so tall and walked so loudly that everybody noticed me. A bleach job I had long wanted but never dared do in the suburbs. A clutch bag, shiny brown leather with gleaming gold clasp, to protect my most treasured belongings: my Bloomingdale's employee charge card and my clove cigarettes.

That's how Sam first saw me, smoking one of those dark cigarettes, sitting at a bar. I was talking to an actor who had his picture and résumé printed on his socks, distorting the image of his face with each flex of his calf muscle.

"It's a great gimmick," the actor was saying. "You wouldn't believe how many agents call me. Next year I'm going to do t-shirts."

The actor had his foot on the bar stool next to me so I could get a close look at his professional credits, but I was looking at Sam. Even across the room, I saw that Sam had gray eyes, the color of the sky before it rains. I'd never seen anyone with gray eyes before.

The actor asked if I'd call him.

"I don't think so," I said, stubbing out my cigarette, closing up the clutch.

"C'mon, Freddy," he called after me, "I'll give you a sock..."

But I was already heading toward Sam.

We spoke very little. I told him I liked his red high-tops and he told me he hated my clogs. I gave him my line about being a comedian and he didn't pretend to believe me.

"Eventually I'd like to do films," I said.

"You'd better hurry," said Sam, "because in a few years there won't be any more films. Everything will be videotaped, even movies."

"I don't like videotape. It's flat."

"What do you know?" he laughed. "You just moved here."

He told me he worked for Andy Warhol, directing a videotaped version of *Interview* magazine.

"Andy's a genius," he said. "A true artist."

"I think his work is shallow."

"What do you know? You just moved here."

I knew I'd go home with him that night. There was something about his small, childlike mouth that I wanted to kiss.

We walked to his apartment, winding through a maze of narrow streets, and though the October air was brisk, we didn't touch until we'd turned onto his beautiful block of brownstones. He took my hand and led me to his small building, pointing out the plaque by the entrance that declared Sam's building a New York Historical Landmark: "No. 14 is a row house designed in the late Italianate style. When erected in 1860, this five-story house was considered the last word in elegance."

Sam lived on the top floor, his apartment dimly lit and cozy, perfect for the first chilly night of autumn. There were postcards taped to his living room wall from Pakistan, Bangladesh, the Taj Mahal.

"Did you travel to India?" I asked.

"My cleaning lady's there on vacation," he explained. "She's a good correspondent."

"She's not much of a cleaning lady," I said, surveying his roomful of empty champagne bottles, unemptied ashtrays, and unfinished cups of cold coffee.

"She's a wonderful cleaning lady," Sam insisted, "but it's been a very long vacation."

I sat on his bed, because it was the only place to sit. There were clothes everywhere, clean clothes spilling out of a laundry bag, getting mixed up with dirty clothes scattered on the floor. The only article of clothing that seemed to be in place was a t-shirt with a Campbell's soup can silk-screened onto it, signed, "To Sam, love, Andy Warhol," hanging on the wall opposite the postcards and framed like a work of art.

Sam turned on the TV and put a tape in the Beta Max, an expensive machine that I'd never seen used outside of a store demonstration at Bloomingdale's.

"Pay attention, Freddy," he told me. "Maybe you'll learn something."

We sat in bed all night watching Andy Warhol and Bianca Jaggar, Andy Warhol and Brooke Shields, Andy Warhol and Calvin Klein. At some point our hands found each other, but we kept our eyes on the screen, staring at the TV like lovers gazing into a fire, each seeing their own series of images dancing in the flames. When the sun came up, Sam put out our fire, ready for sleep, but he opened his eyes as I pressed my mouth against his, dragging my lips across his face to his ear.

"It's too late or too early or something," he whispered. "I can't..."

"You don't have to," I said. "I'll do it all."

I had not yet made love in New York City, and I had never made love like this before. The men I'd known in Maryland were middle-aged, older than Sam and much older than I, a teacher from my high school, a customer from the mall. We'd meet late at night in parking lots, the ice-skating rink in summer or the swimming pool in winter, always off-season. The other car was usually bigger than mine, so I'd slide into the passenger's seat, the driver undoing his pants and pushing my head toward his crotch. I gasped and gagged, my head hitting the steering wheel as the windows steamed with the driver's desire, no room left for mine. But Sam never made me touch him: his stormy gray eyes looked startled when I did, as though no one had ever devoted himself to pleasing Sam. He didn't try to reciprocate, and I didn't need him to, freed by his lack of expectation, liberated by his passivity. I wanted to take care of Sam, to please him, to part the clouds I saw in his eyes and find some light there.

■ ■ ■ ■

We stayed in bed for days. It was hard to tell day from night in that room, but the TV was constantly on, providing some sort of structure for our time. Sam didn't cook and though I did, I found no food in his refrigerator, so all meals were ordered out, Chinese, Mexican, Indian in honor of the maid. We ate in bed, tossing the take-out cartons on the floor where I supposed they'd remain until the cleaning lady returned from her trip. I wondered how long we'd remain in bed, knowing I should call Bloomingdale's and lie about being sick. I got as far as lifting the red phone with my feet, punching the number with my toes as I imagined the gourmet-food counter and the constant mob of angry housewives and Japanese tourists screaming, "What is chutney?" The Bloomingdale's in Maryland had seemed like New York to me, but here, at the flagship store, I felt as if I were back in a mall, far away from the City, and I hung up the phone when on the fifteenth ring an operator finally answered.

Sam made no calls and never received one, though on the third morning, someone from Andy Warhol's office came with croissants and hot coffee to wake Sam up and take him to work. Sam shared his coffee with me while Andy's assistant sat at the foot of the bed, like a reporter covering John and Yoko's bed-in for peace, not seeming to care or even notice that I was naked. I assumed the assistant had been to many of these bed-ins.

Bloomingdale's didn't send anyone to my apartment, only a message on my answering service to inform me that my employee-credit-card privileges and I had been terminated. Fifty hours a week on a sales clerk's salary couldn't quite cover the rent on my new apartment in the greasiest part of Hell's Kitchen, so I decided to do what struggling performers are supposed to do, wait on tables, where more money could be made in less time. I started my job search at an elegant French restaurant I'd noticed near Bloomingdale's.

"Are you hiring?" I asked the maitre d'. He looked up from the napkins he was folding, his dark eyes glaring at me from behind his bifocals.

"Do you have New York restaurant experience?" he said.

"Absolutely," I answered, trying not to sound too eager, too nice, too new in the City.

"Then fill this out completely," he told me, eyeing me suspiciously as he handed me an application.

I sat down at a little table by the bar and opened my clutch bag, taking out a pen, a clove cigarette, and packs of matches I'd collected from various restaurants in New York: a cafe in the Village, a theatre hangout in midtown, a coffee shop in SoHo. I turned my back to the maitre d' so he couldn't see me copying restaurant names and phone numbers from matchbook covers onto the application as my "Previous Experience," with made-up dates of employment and phony supervisors' names.

The maitre d' led me to a small office that doubled as a coat check room. I sat down, surrounded by fur coats though it was not yet Halloween, unsure of who I was waiting for until a large woman looking like Peggy Lee popped her head through the coat check window, my application in her hand.

"I'm the owner," she said. "Do you like children?"

"I love kids," I told her, relieved that she hadn't asked about the restaurants I'd listed.

"I loathe them," she said slowly. "They're not allowed in my establishment under any circumstances. Get it?"

"Sure..."

"Then you've got the job, Frederick."

"It's Freddy," I corrected her.

"Don't argue with me, Frederick," said the owner, tossing my application onto her desk and disappearing from the coat check window, the end of the Peggy Lee Show.

Sam called me the next afternoon as I was leaving for my first day of work.

"Scurrying off to Bloomie's, are we?" he asked.

I told him about my new waitering job, full of pride at the New York savvy I had used to get it.

"That was stupid," said Sam. "What if they call those other restaurants?"

"I'll be no worse off than I was. It's a gamble."

He told me he wanted to see me again, and we made a date for that weekend, though it was no different from our first meeting, not much of a date. When I arrived at his apartment, the door was ajar so Sam didn't have to get out of bed to let me in. There were more empty take-out cartons on the floor, perhaps from a bed-in more recent than ours, and though the only light was coming from the TV screen, I could see he'd received another postcard from the cleaning lady, "Greetings from Sri Lanka." I took off my clothes, laid the clutch bag on his night table for easy access to my clove cigarettes, and slid under the covers with Sam. He reached over and held my hand, barely saying hello, his eyes fixed on the TV, where Andy Warhol was taking a cooking lesson from Julia Child.

We spent many evenings like this. I liked the way Sam held me tight all night long, as if he would never let go. His arms felt comforting after a grueling week of waiting tables at an elegant

French restaurant that didn't seem so elegant when the maitre d' was yelling, "You'll never learn to make a good cappuccino until you put your heart in your work."

My attempts at comedy were also halfhearted. After standing for eight hours in a tuxedo stained with that night's dinner specials, I hardly felt funny, and most of the audiences who saw my ten-minute set did not laugh. I didn't tell Sam this: I didn't tell Sam anything and he never asked, wrapping me in his arms while he watched Andy. He had the same response to whatever I said: "What do you know? You just moved here." So I'd wait silently for Andy to leave, waiting to make love to Sam. That's when he would look at me, his eyes like two rain clouds hovering over me, blocking the sun.

Still, late at night after leaving the restaurant or bombing at a club, I'd long to see Sam. I hated coming home to my Ninth Avenue high-rise with a whorehouse on the fifth floor, riding in the elevator next to nervous johns, and sometimes the girls themselves: white girls wearing hot pants on the coldest November nights, black girls with hair bleached more blonde than mine, an Asian girl half my height and clad in rabbit who'd learned my name from my doorman, her pimp.

"Freddy, there's quite a discount for guys who live in the building," she'd say, leaning on the DOOR OPEN button when the elevator reached five and stroking her furry jacket.

At moments like those, I thought of Sam's bed. I would imagine his white cotton sheets like a blanket of snow, the kind you're supposed to build if you're caught in a blizzard. A blanket of snow to keep you warm, insulate you, help you survive the storm.

■ ■ ■ ■

The restaurant was too French to attract families with young children, and it was over a month before two tourists from Texas showed up for Sunday brunch with their baby and a toddler. They'd made a reservation, but the maitre d' was in the kitchen with the owner, dealing with a dissatisfied customer's omelet, so

I sat the family in my section at an out-of-the-way table, the mother gathering their coats for me to check, the two-year-old's ski jacket, the newborn's stroller. The children were well behaved, no noise coming from the back of my section, and Peggy Lee was busy yelling at the bartender to make weaker mimosas and riding the busboy to turn over tables by clearing customers' plates if they were anywhere near finished. She still hadn't noticed the family as I served them their food, until she went to her office to use the phone.

"Whose is this?" she asked from inside the coat check room, and though a table nearby looked up to see who was speaking, no one else heard her.

"Whose goddamn stroller is this?" she repeated loudly, heaving the stroller out the coat check window, sending it soaring through the air, the entire room watching as it crashed to the floor, immediately followed by a tiny ski jacket.

"Excuse me," said the man, his wife clinging to their children, "but I think that was our stroller."

It was also my job. I turned my checks over to the maitre d' and left the restaurant, walking to Fifth Avenue, where the store windows had been recently redecorated for Christmas. The sun was blindingly bright, the way it can be on very cold days, and as I went window to window, perusing the jewels at Tiffany's, studying the glass figurines at Steuben that glowed under spotlights like ice refusing to melt, I felt scared of New York City. Scared about my ability to support myself. Scared I'd never have an answer for Sam when he asked, "What do you know, you just moved here." And then, I heard trumpets blaring "Joy to the World." Sidewalk traffic stopped, taxis slowed down, searching for the source of the music. It seemed to be coming from heaven, so I looked up and there, dozens of stories above me on the terrace of an unfinished building, were five trumpeters.

But Sam hadn't heard them: Sam had not changed, barely responding when I told him about my day.

"Don't you have any interest in my life outside your bedroom, Sam?" I asked. "Minor details like being fired, having to get a new job three weeks before Christmas. Do they interest you at all?"

"No," he said, "not really."

I saw a flicker in his eyes, but this time I turned away, not to the TV like Sam, but to the wall with the bedroom's one, covered-up window. I wanted to tear down the canvas screen and see the world that Sam had shut out.

I didn't make love to Sam that night.

As I was getting dressed early the next morning, he told me he was spending a month in Rio de Janeiro.

"I leave next week," he said.

"You'll be away for Christmas."

"That's why I'm going," said Sam. "I hate Christmas."

I had my coat on now. I picked up the clutch and headed for the door.

"I won't see you till next year," I said.

"Yeah, I'll let you know when I'm back. And Freddy," he called after me, "lose the bag. It looks real stupid."

I ran down the five flights of stairs and out of his building, and leaned against the historical landmark plaque, unable to breathe, unable to move for fear that someone would point at my clogs, or stare at my bleached hair, or laugh at the clutch. When I finally took the first step, I never wanted to see Sam again.

■ ■ ■ ■

I didn't see Sam for a few years, and during that time, I did lose the bag, at first forgetting to grab it as I left the house. Soon it looked more natural sitting on my dresser than it did clutched under my arm, so I stopped carrying it. My hair also looked more natural, no longer bleached but highlighted, subtly tinted gold in sections and skillfully blended with my light brown color. Even the clogs went, replaced by a pair of Reeboks. I found a restaurant that liked children and me, where Claire walked into my life, and when she walked out of it, I dumped comedy for drama, enrolling in an acting class with a famous teacher who'd recently undergone est training.

"Thank you," she would say when I finished a monologue, "for having the generosity to share your gift, the courage to confront your ability, and the talent to take us into your soul."

"Thank you," I'd tell her, "for teaching me to mine the treasures within."

Then members of the class would thank me for letting them learn by my mistakes, and I thanked them for creating an environment where I felt safe enough to make mistakes. By the end of each class we were always tearful. By the end of the term, I was cast in an off-off-Broadway play.

When the director told me I got the part, I wanted to call Sam. I'd thought about calling him many times, and often, late at night, I'd walk by his elegant brownstone, wishing I could climb in bed and bury myself in the snow with Sam's hand holding mine. The plaque by the door was as far as I went, running my fingers over the engraved words like a blind person reading braille, looking up at the windows and wondering if one of them was the window I could never see out of.

I met other men at the bar where I'd first seen Sam, but no matter who I was talking to, rich or handsome, I kept an eye on the door, watching for Sam and his clouds to roll in.

A few months after my play had closed, he did.

"Now you do know something," I told myself as Sam walked toward me. "You know you're an actor in New York City."

Sam knew that too. He had read the *New York Times* review in which I'd been mentioned favorably enough to get myself a good agent.

"Sorry I didn't see the show," said Sam.

"That's okay," I told him, remembering the many hours I'd spent watching Sam's work, watching Andy.

"You never call me," he said.

"It's been two years. Did you just notice?"

"I've missed you."

"What do you miss?" I asked. "You didn't know me."

"I knew you, Freddy, and I knew how much you liked me," Sam said, "but you were another stray who'd come to the City, and the worst thing I could have done for you was to take you in. You had to do it on your own, just like I did."

"I'm not a stray anymore, Sam," I said, though the words sounded false, and I wished I'd carried the review in my pocket to remind myself that I belonged here.

"Something's changed," he said. "You look incredible."

Sam had never seen me in the summer before: I was golden tan, golden blond, golden boy. He took me dancing to a club called the Anvil in the basement of a seedy meat-packing-district motel, but we were stopped at the door by a bouncer in black leather chaps and a biker's cap.

"I can't let you in looking like that," the bouncer told me.

"What's wrong with the way I look?" I asked him.

"You're too clean," said Sam. "Do something to yourself. Mess up your hair. At least you don't have that damn bag."

"Leave my bag alone," I told him, untucking my shirt and rumpling my clothes until the bouncer deemed me disheveled enough to enter. "I don't know why you'd want to go into a place like this."

The small, smoky room was filled with men in various uniforms: police uniforms, army uniforms, motorcycle-gang uniforms. Most of them had big, well-built bodies, though they chatted and giggled like little boys at a Halloween party. Sam and I danced wildly on the tiny dance floor, whirling and spinning and jumping around. Soon we were surrounded by the uniformed men and a few drag queens, smiling as they watched us dance, like guests at a wedding watching the bride and groom.

"Does the rest of the Brady Bunch know you can dance like that?" asked one of the army officers.

"There's a lot they don't know," I answered.

At dawn, we took our dance back to Sam's apartment. The floor was clear of clothes and take-out cartons. I wondered if that meant no bed-ins.

"Is your cleaning lady back?" I asked.

"No," he told me, pointing to the postcards. There must have been over thirty, from the Middle East, the Orient, the Soviet Union. "I can't keep up with her travel schedule."

"Do I smell coffee?" I said.

"It's the new coffeemaker my mother sent me," he said. "State-of-the-art with a timer, but the timer's broken, so it brews on a whim. Would you like a cup?"

I shook my head, reading the postcards, looking at the signed Campbell's soup t-shirt. Sam came up behind me and wrapped me in his arms, turning me around and kissing me. I did not respond, so he kissed me again, gently biting my lower lip.

"Show me your teeth," I whispered.

"What?"

"I've never seen your teeth. Even when you smile, they're hidden."

I put my hands on his face, pulling his upper lip, revealing the teeth of a child: tiny, fragile, white. I ran my finger along them, and he grabbed hold of it with his baby teeth, biting down hard, but it didn't hurt. I knew those teeth couldn't hurt me.

We went to bed, playing in the snow until we were both exhausted. Sam fell asleep before me, his body pressed against mine, his arm gripping me so tight I could barely breathe.

I woke up to the smell of coffee and Sam, two of the most comforting smells I knew, but this time I had phone calls that had to be made, using Sam's red phone to check in with my agent. He'd scheduled me an audition for a Dr. Pepper commercial, so I couldn't do a three-day bed-in, and though Sam wished me good luck, he didn't ask how it had gone when he called me the following week. I didn't tell him I'd booked it, but sometimes my commercial would come on while we were watching TV, and Sam would turn up the volume, listening to me talk about soft drinks, and later about aspirin, then antiperspirant, and I wondered why Sam only allowed my voice to fill his bedroom filtered through the television.

I made enough money from commercials to move to a brownstone, not as elegant as Sam's, near Central Park and away from the whores. The building was owned by an artist who lived on the top floor, and he'd decorated the stairways with his bold, colorful paintings, lending me one to hang over my fireplace. Sam showed no interest in seeing my new apartment, and I grew less and less interested in seeing his: the world he blocked out no longer seemed unsafe, a place I needed to hide from. Occasionally I spent the night, but we rarely made love anymore or watched Andy, or stayed up past the eleven o'clock news: John Lennon bleeding, Natalie Wood drowning, me suffocating under a blanket of snow.

■ ■ ■ ■

Andy Warhol's TV show never made it into *TV Guide* but my name did, for my portrayal of a homicidal cross-dresser stalked by the lowest-rated detective on prime time that season. I assumed Sam hadn't seen the show: I hadn't seen Sam since I met and moved in with a man who listened if I spoke. That's who I was watching the news with when Andy's death was announced, the first time in several years I'd sat in bed and watched Andy Warhol, though his picture was always in the newspaper or a magazine, reminding me of Sam, our bed-ins, my early days in the City. The restaurant where I'd first waited tables was under new ownership, trying to overcome the past with a "We welcome children!" sign in the window, and often I'd go out of my way to walk by Sam's apartment, imagining a second plaque by the door that declared it my personal landmark.

Sam showed up in my dreams that night wearing the Campbell's soup can t-shirt, and the next morning, on the set of the soap opera in which I had a small but recurring role, everyone was talking about Andy Warhol.

"Do you think it was AIDS?" a makeup man asked me, dusting powder on my face.

"I think it was a postsurgical medical mishap," I told him.

"This makeup must be good," he laughed. "You sound like a doctor."

"For the next few weeks," I said, "then I'm another unemployed actor."

All my scenes were taped on the soap's hospital set, getting on and off an elevator that moved nowhere, dashing down the hall holding the patient's blank chart. I played a specialist in the leading lady's rare and nameless disease, and now that her contract had been renegotiated, total recovery seemed certain. My days were numbered, though she was still in a coma, bolting out of bed between takes and tearing the fake I.V. from her arm, smoking a cigarette with hairdressers huddled around her. I thought of the real hospitals I'd visited, my agent, an early AIDS victim, quarantined in the Intensive Care Unit with mummified nurses and food workers too frightened to feed him. Now there were AIDS wards, one of which was decorated with the same exuberant paintings that once hung in my brownstone, a legacy to the ward from my landlord-artist, who had died there.

Neither my boyfriend nor I had been tested, and though we'd had sex only with each other for the past five years, I worried about what went on before we met, before we knew how dangerous desire could be. I'd started checking the obituaries long before Andy Warhol's death for names of forgotten friends and ex-lovers, and though Sam's never appeared there, he also wasn't mentioned in any of the stories about Andy. Was there still a TV show? Was there still a Sam? He'd never been listed in the phone book, but I remembered his number, and though I knew he might have moved to another apartment, to another city, I dialed it, my boyfriend asleep in the other room as I waited for someone — for Sam — to answer. I imagined him lifting the red phone with his feet, but when his voice came on the line, it was a recording. Still, his voice sounded the same and I was relieved to hear it, leaving my new phone number and a jumbled message about Andy.

Sam called me back from one of the few hospitals I hadn't been to, and I brought him flowers when I visited the next night.

"I don't know where you're going to put them," he said. The little table next to his bed was covered with medications, toiletries, crumpled Kleenex covering the telephone. I made room for the flowers and sat on the edge of his bed, the television suspended from a beam above us. Several "Get Well" cards were taped to the wall: I wondered if they were all from his cleaning lady.

"Forgive my hair," said Sam, running his fingers over his bald scalp, "I can't do a thing with it."

"We have wigs where I work," I said, looking into his gray eyes, which seemed to be the last feature left on his gaunt face. "I could bring you one. Redhead, blond..."

"It doesn't matter," he said. "This hospital's not glamorous like the hospital you hang out in."

"You've seen me on the show?" I asked.

"There's not much else to do," he told me, pointing up at the TV. "Didn't I tell you everything would be videotaped?"

"Everything's not videotaped, Sam. I happen to be doing a show that is."

"What do you know?" said Sam, taking my hand, the touch that had once brought me comfort now causing me fear.

I sat with Sam, watching TV until visiting hours were over.

"I'll be back," I said.

"No more flowers," he told me. "There's no space, and it's not like home where I can toss things on the floor."

"I don't want to show up empty-handed."

"Bring me a shaving kit," said Sam. "Something to keep my stuff in."

I knew what I would bring. My boyfriend watched silently as I pulled boxes out of our storage closet until I found the trunk where I'd packed away the life I'd led prior to our relationship. The lock was jammed, so I jimmied it open, dozens of *Playbill*s spilling out, along with warranties from appliances I no longer owned. I found it buried near the bottom, reeking of clove cigarettes, the leather still lustrous but the gold clasp broken.

I made Sam close his eyes before I gave him his gift, placing the clutch in his hands. He lifted it to his nose.

"Is it supposed to be an air freshener?" he asked.

"Open your eyes and see," I told him.

I thought Sam would laugh, but he didn't, and though he smiled so broadly I could see his baby teeth, his rain-cloud eyes seemed ready to burst.

"Not exactly a shaving kit," I said. "I can get you something else if you..."

"No," he said quietly, hugging it to his chest. "I want this bag."

The clutch sat on his bedside table, next to the clock, the phone, the flowers I brought nightly though he told me not to. Sam watched my show every day, and as the leading lady regained consciousness, Sam began to lose his, fading in and out of conversations, mistaking me for people I didn't know, perhaps other bed-in partners. My boyfriend had dinner waiting when I got home, and somehow we discussed Sam's declining health without discussing its implications.

I missed Sam's death by a half hour. A young, inexperienced director caused the taping to run overtime and Sam couldn't wait. The nurses knew me by now, and they let me into his room to see the body. His eyes were wide open, staring right at me, and I closed them, kissing his forehead and taking the clutch with me. Outside, I stood in a short line waiting for a cab. Flurries had started, barely enough to notice but too much for the woman in front of me, who was already complaining of icy streets and slushy sidewalks.

"Don't you hate snow?" she asked, and the rest of the taxi line nodded, comparing weather reports.

"Less than an inch predicted."

"A bit more in the suburbs."

"Not supposed to stick."

A single flake landed on my leather bag and I covered the clutch with my coat, shielding it from the flurries as I shivered in the evening air, for though the others in line agreed this snow would be long gone by morning, I was expecting a blizzard, wondering how long I'd survive under a blanket of snow without Sam's arms to keep me warm.

Fallingwater

The woman at the Ramada Inn says she has lost my parents.

"They were here a minute ago, checking in," she tells me. "I turned around to answer the phone, and now they're gone. It's baffling."

What baffles me is that they've shown up. In the ten years since I left home for New York City, they've never visited or seen me in a show, yet here they are in the mountains of Pennsylvania at a rural Ramada Inn — or were, until they disappeared — to watch me star in a summer-stock sex farce. The audience of locals laughs at the double entendres, the dropped drawers, but the only aspect of the play that amuses me is the title, *Why Not Stay for Breakfast?*, and I can't imagine my parents will stay for the second act. I haven't ordered their tickets for tonight's performance: I assumed they'd cancel, citing the failing health of my elderly father, their elderly dog, the elderly car, but I know by the clerk's description that they've made it as far as the hotel.

"A white-haired man smoking a long cigar and a redheaded woman with a thick, Southern accent," she says. "I'm writing this down, sending the bellboy on a search."

Dick Scanlan

The bellboy will have a hard time. The hotel is much larger than the house I grew up in, and it sometimes took hours for my father and all five children to find my mother, each searching a section of the house, checking every closet, the attic, the pantry. On summer evenings, the search would spill outside to the yard, each of us equipped with a flashlight. "We've got to find your mother," my father told us, and eventually we would, hiding in the azaleas or behind a yellow forsythia bush, smiling like a little girl playing hide-and-seek. "Marge," my father would say, "this is the limit. This really is the limit."

I give the hotel clerk my phone number.

"Would you have my parents call me once they're found?"

"Of course," she says, "and they will be. I promise you that on behalf of all of us at the Ramada."

"Thanks," I tell her. "I'm not worried." I hang up the phone, realizing my lack of concern must seem strange to the clerk, but I know my parents will resurface and I know why they've disappeared: my mother's Southern accent emerges only when she's drinking, her disappearing act performed only when she's drunk.

She used to go solo until a stroke left my father almost blind and unable to look for her. Now she takes him along. He's probably sitting with my mother at some dark bar, unaware that he's joined her act, the disappearing duet, already forgetting why they've come to Pennsylvania. My father remembers every lawerly phrase and legal theory he knew before the stroke, able to quote case histories as though he was still a third-year law student, but he is dependent on my mother to tell him which day it is, when he last ate, what the names of his newest grandchildren are.

The phone rings. I am expecting my mother's drunken drawl, but the voice I hear is strong and Long Island.

"Did they arrive?" asks Mark.

"Briefly," I say, "fleeing the Ramada Inn during registration."

"Had she been drinking?" he asks.

"What do you think?"

"I thought they were coming with your sister," he says.

"Separate cars," I explain. "My parents can't handle Katie's husband for 290 miles."

"I don't know how your mother handled a car in that condition," says Mark.

"She's lucky that way," I tell him. "She never gets caught."

"Freddy, she could have killed someone."

"A child," I say. "Drunk drivers always seem to kill children."

A nurse comes to draw more of Mark's blood, and I hear her in the background as Mark hangs up, her voice gravelly yet sweet. Tomorrow I'll be able to match it to a face, along with the doctors and social workers Mark's met since the summer flu he was fighting last week sent him to the hospital with a 106° fever, turning into the kind of pneumonia that means AIDS. There was a message waiting for me after the show, and while the rest of the cast went to a Fourth of July party, I tried to reach Mark in the emergency room, sending word that I'd given the producer my one-week's notice, that I was on my way home. Sitting in bed I could hear the muffled sound of fireworks, like a distant battle, but outside my window all I saw were stars. I looked for the North Star and both dippers, but I can never find them, no matter how many times Mark points them out to me. Still, I searched all night, afraid to close my eyes, afraid to dream of the future, and when the sun came up, I called my mother, always her best in the early morning, after a cup of coffee and before any bourbon.

"AIDS?" she gasped, as if AIDS had never occurred to her, though she knows I'm gay, knows Mark is my lover. "My God."

I could picture her alone in the kitchen, my father asleep upstairs. She had many questions that I was unable to answer, unable to speak.

"I'm coming to see you," she whispered, "to hold you and tell you over and over again how much I love you." It sounded like a lullaby to me, with lyrics that comfort without making sense, the melody more important than the meaning.

▪ ▪ ▪ ▪

I spread a sheet over the grass, coating my legs and arms with suntan oil that smells like a piña colada, overwhelming the scent of mountain wildflowers. My skin grows warm from the sun, wet from humidity, and though I've read about the harmful effects of ultraviolet rays, I'm thinking short term, risking wrinkles in the future for a tan by tomorrow night, a healthy glow that will make Mark feel better and keep me from getting sick. I picture us on our separate sheets, me in the sun and Mark in the hospital, his face drawn and pale, or perhaps flushed with fever. His voice hasn't changed, native New Yorker, tough when nurses are near, tender late at night, and until I see him in a hospital gown, attached to an I.V., I'll wonder if there's been a mistake, a misdiagnosis, a false positive.

Inside the phone is ringing. I run tiptoe over the prickly grass, trying to turn the doorknob with my lotioned fingers, trying to grasp the phone in my greasy hands.

"Were you sleeping?" asks my brother-in-law, though it is early afternoon, a banker's version of life in the theatre.

"No, Vincent. I've been up for minutes," I say. "Did you and Katie just get here?"

"Katherine and I arrived a bit ago," he says, referring to everyone by the name on their birth certificate, keeping his distance from our family as if not sure he wants to be a part of it, "but there was a mix-up regarding your parents..."

"She did her Houdini," Katie calls from the background. She has little tolerance for my mother's alcoholism, and no tolerance for alcohol, which cost Katie two jobs, her first husband, and, in a drunk-driving accident, almost her life. She hasn't been behind the wheel and she hasn't been under the influence since.

"No need for alarm," Vincent tells me. "Your parents have been located, Frederick. They'd wandered down the road for a soda or something."

This makes me laugh, and I hear Katie laughing too. Vincent seems irritated, but he's been married to my sister for only six months: he doesn't know the rules yet. We are not silent about my mother's drinking, entertaining each other with tales of her passing out facefirst in the mashed potatoes or on the dance floors at my sister's two weddings. We use words like "loaded," "hooched," "blotto," and we make it funnier by imitating my mother's slurred Southern speech. Each of us can do this imitation, but I, the youngest and the actor, do the best, and I would sometimes be dragged out of bed during my oldest brother's parties to perform on command my impersonation of my mother, crossing my eyes, weaving through the room, making guests laugh.

"Your mother needs time to freshen up," says Vincent, and Katie grabs the phone.

"She's toasted," Katie tells me. "Lit. Give us an hour to pump her with coffee and we'll come get you."

I give her directions to the farmhouse I've lived in this summer, sharing a showerless bathroom with the cast.

"What little of Mom's mutterings I could understand seemed to involve taking you to lunch," says my sister, "then Vincent wants to see Fallingwater. Do you remember how to get there?"

"Mark drove," I say, "but I think I know the way."

I sent picture postcards of Fallingwater to all my friends and everyone in my family, telling them that my tour of the famous house had been far more exciting than the previous night's opening of *Why Not Stay for Breakfast?* Still, I doubt my family will like the look of Fallingwater, comparing it to the newer models that now surround my parents' colonial-style home.

"Modern houses," my mother once complained to Mark, the only architect she knows, "they're all roof."

"You're right," he told her, "in most instances."

But not Fallingwater, a house that Frank Lloyd Wright built over a waterfall for a family, two parents and a son. It seems to grow out of the forest surrounding it, as tall as the tallest tree, as sturdy as the hardest stone. Inside, the greenish gray floors glisten like wet rock, and the furniture is built into the walls: polished wooden surfaces and long, low-backed sofas covered in thick fabrics, the kind you're not afraid to sit on, the kind you could nap on during a stormy afternoon. There are windows everywhere, and the sound of the waterfall is always present, rumbling under the house like the hum of a well-tuned engine.

■ ■ ■ ■

It is my mother's car but Vincent is driving, honking the horn and sipping something 7-Eleven-ish from a huge pink cup, my mother slumped behind him in the backseat. Vincent is too fat to fit comfortably in the driver's seat, but I've seen every size and shape behind the wheel of my mother's car — concerned neighbors, sixteen-year-old salesclerks, eleven-year-old me propped up on telephone books, driving to the bus stop to get my father.

"Marge," he'd say as he stepped off the bus and saw me sitting on the Yellow Pages, "this is the limit. This really is the limit."

I call from the bathroom window, "Be there in a minute," and inspect myself in the old mirror, a set piece from another summer's show. Today's sun brought out the green in my hazel eyes and the gold in my hair, the only blond in our family of redheads, the only one who tans. "I'm not sure where you came from," my mother used to say, "but I'm sure glad you're here."

Vincent honks again as I open the front door, and all of them wave. My father doesn't know where I am, waving in the wrong direction until I come to his window and put my hand on his shoulder.

"Good to see you, son," he says, patting my hand.

I slide into the backseat. Katie kisses my cheek and my mother takes both my hands, holding them too tight, her drunken grip always painful.

"Mom," I say, "you're hurting me."

"I'm sorry, hon. I'm just so happy to see you."

Katie rolls her eyes as my mother loosens her grip.

"You look handsome," says my mother, her accent slurred and Southern, "brown as a berry."

"Explain that expression, Mrs. Donovan," says Vincent, slowly pulling out of the driveway. He's not ready for Mom or Marge or anything more than Mrs. "I've never understood it. Aren't berries red?"

My mother does not answer: she is staring at me, her hair thick and auburn at sixty, her cheekbones high and chiseled, her eyes the color of emeralds. She is still beautiful, though there are wrinkles lining her face, not the kind that come from smiling too much, and her clothes are dirty, as they always are when she's drunk, her short-sleeved blouse the color of the sun viewed through filthy, spotted sunglasses.

Vincent drives carefully up and down the steep mountain roads that lead to Fallingwater, hand over hand on the turns, gently pumping the brakes, as though driving is the one sport he excels at, the one protection he can offer Katie, who never talks about her nearly fatal crash. He comes to a complete halt before sipping his drink, taking quick swigs of his big beverage at every red light or stop sign, irritated at having to balance it in his lap.

"I have a cup container clipped to my car door," he tells the rearview mirror, and I'm sure he wanted to drive his big boat to Fallingwater, my mother refusing for some drunk and stubborn reason. "And cruise control. All cars should have cruise control."

"How's Mark?" asks Katie, not interested in cruise control, none of my family interested in cars.

"Sick," I tell her. "Very sick, though he's responding to the treatment for pneumonia and might be out of the hospital by next week."

"Then what happens?" I hear concern in Katie's voice, but she has my father's eyes, small and brown and unexpressive. The rest of her is a miniature version of my mother, flaming hair and fine features, under five feet tall. She is petite, as my mother would be if she didn't drink, for I've never seen my mother eat an entire meal or even a whole sandwich, usually ordering cups of soup that she doesn't finish.

"Then we take a trip, if Mark's doctor gives the okay. We've always wanted to see Italy. Seems like a good time to go."

"It's an expensive time to go, Frederick," says Vincent. "The dollar is weak, so you'll get the most for your money right here at home."

"Why not spend a week in Maine," suggests my father.

"I don't know if Mark will be well enough to spend a week anywhere," I say.

"I can't believe it," says Katie, shaking her head. "He seemed fine at our wedding."

"He seemed fine when he visited me last month," I tell her. "Sleeping more than usual, but I attributed that to being overworked. He does twelve-hour days when I'm out of town."

"That's why Mark's a success," says my father. "Good on the job, and wonderful at the wheel."

Vincent is unnerved by my father's compliment, as though he's competing against Mark for Best In-law Driver, but Mark earned my father's vote the day of Katie and Vincent's wedding, driving my mother's car through a light snow that turned into a storm soon after we left my parents' house. My mother's car was not equipped with snow tires or chains, and though it took over an hour to get us to the church, Mark got us there without a skid.

"Mark's a wonderful person," my mother says quietly. "I love him dearly."

I remember the first time I brought Mark home. We'd met a few months before at a bar, which I described to my mother as a party. I'd never brought a man home before, and though my parents seemed uncomfortable that first night, my mother put us in the same bedroom. Mark's an early riser, like my mother, and by the time my father and I came down for breakfast the next morning, Mark had fixed their TV antenna so they'd get better reception, fixed the wiring in the dining room so they could use the chandelier, fixed the flue in the fireplace so they could have fires. My parents watched in amazement as Mark refinished and rewired, building them the bookcases they'd talked about for years. Near the end of the weekend my mother called Mark into the garage to look at a broken door, and when they were alone she held his hand in her drunken grip and said, "Thank you for giving Freddy the support he needs up there in New York. I was never able to give him what he needed."

Vincent is hungry.

"Is there a restaurant at Fallingwater?" he asks.

"No," I tell him, "but Mark and I stopped at a diner called Babe's. The burgers were great."

"Burgers?" says Vincent. "Surely there's a McDonald's or a Burger King nearby."

"I don't think so," I say. "Conveniently located fast food wasn't one of Frank Lloyd Wright's priorities."

Vincent is skeptical about eating at a place called Babe's, still grumbling when we see the beat-up sign standing next to the small restaurant, no bigger than a trailer. He pulls into Babe's graveled parking lot and, as if he is taking his driver's test, does a perfect three-point turn before parallel-parking my parents' car.

▪ ▪ ▪ ▪

Babe's is empty and cool inside, a standing fan creating a breeze. The three tables are covered with clean, red-checkered tablecloths, the home-baked pies arranged in a case exactly as they were when Mark and I ate here. I recognize the waitress's frizzy gray hair and clean pink hands as she pushes two of the three tables together to seat our party of five.

"I've seen you," she says, giving me a menu, and I wonder if Mark and I were her most recent customers, if anyone's eaten at Babe's in the six weeks since our lunch, "at the Playhouse, in ... oh..."

"Why Not Stay for Breakfast?" I say.

My sister laughs.

"You've seen it too?" the waitress asks her. "Isn't it funny?"

"We're seeing it tonight," says Katie. "I just get a kick out of the title."

"Wait till you see the play," says our waitress. "But I don't want to give away the plot, so let's talk about lunch."

I don't open my menu; I know I want what Mark and I had. Katie and my father order tuna sandwiches, and Vincent chooses the meat-loaf special, with soup, salad, candied carrots, rolls, and a strawberry shake.

"And you, ma'am?" the waitress asks my mother.

My mother is silent, leering at the menu, leering at the waitress, then back at the menu.

"Marge," my father says, "do you want some soup?"

"Absolutely not," she says, as if insulted. "I am trying to decide between a sausage pizza or an order of french fries."

Katie takes over. "Bring her a cup of coffee and a cup of soup," she says, and the waitress heads toward the kitchen, stopped by my mother's loud voice.

"'Scuse me," she slurs, " but I'm still trying to decide between a sausage pizza or an order of french fries."

"Why not get both?" I whisper to Katie.

My mother hears me.

"I will," says my mother, "I want both."

"Should I bring extra plates for the pizza?" asks our waitress.

"No," my mother snaps. "It's all mine."

The food comes quickly, the waitress setting the large pizza in front of my mother, the french fries to the side.

"I wish I had my camera," says Katie, as my mother smacks the ketchup bottle, spanking it like a naughty child until a blob of ketchup lands on the tablecloth, nowhere near the fries. She daintily dips, then tastes a french fry.

The pizza she attacks, tearing off the hot cheese and sausage and eating it out of her hand like a caveman, coating her face, her fingers, her wedding ring with tomato sauce, dropping sausage on her yellow blouse. She opens and closes her eyes as she eats, as though she is chewing with them, her lips pursed and in constant motion, side to side, up and down, unable to decide where they belong on her face. I mirror my mother's contortions, mimicking her for my sister.

"I don't see what's so funny," says Vincent, embarrassed by my mother, pleased by his food. My father looks helpless, as if he wants to get angry but has forgotten how, and Katie and I keep laughing, making my mother laugh too, cheese and sausage shooting from her mouth.

"Marge," growls my father, "for God's sake..."

Katie and I calm down, but my mother is still laughing, and I wonder if she knows that we were laughing at her, that she's laughing at herself. She starts to choke on a piece of pizza, and the waitress rushes over with a glass of water, my father slapping my mother on the back until she can breathe.

"Thank you," my father tells the waitress. "I apologize for this mess."

"Pizza and spareribs," she says, handing my mother a warm, damp cloth. "Just one way to eat them. With your fingers."

She clears our plates. Only Vincent's is empty, and he is eyeing the pies.

"Are they as delicious as they look?" he asks me.

"I don't know," I say. "Mark and I didn't order dessert."

I had wanted to try a piece of Babe's coconut cream, but Mark was too excited about taking me to Fallingwater, the house he'd studied in college and visited many times since, the house that inspired his career.

"Fallingwater has no foundation," he told me during lunch, briefing me for our tour. "It's built over water."

"How does it stay up?" I asked.

"Balance," said Mark, holding my hand under the table. "All the pieces of the house rest against each other in perfect balance, stronger than any concrete could ever be."

We leave the waitress a large tip.

"Good luck," she says to me, "with the play."

I take a cup of coffee with me despite the heat of the day, suddenly very tired. Vincent buys a candy bar for the road, and we ride in silence the few remaining miles to Fallingwater.

■ ■ ■ ■

The parking lot is crowded.

"All these people came to see that?" asks Vincent, pointing to a large, wooden structure.

"That's a faux Fallingwater rest area, where you buy the tickets," I tell him. "Mark hated it. The real house is hidden behind those trees."

Vincent wants the best possible parking space, dropping us off at the ticket booth and stalking the front rows of the lot, ready to pounce at the first sign of another car's departure. Katie and I find a bench for our parents, and we join the crowd waiting to take the next tour.

"Mark and I must have come off-season," I say. "There were a handful of people here."

"Did he take you on a private tour?" she asks. "He probably knows every inch of the place."

"They make you stick with a guide, but Mark knew more about the house than she did, so he took over, talking about cantilevers, glass density, sandstone excavation."

The line starts to move. I help my mother off the bench, holding onto her arm, as Katie guides my father. Vincent appears from inside the gift shop, sipping a carton of chocolate milk.

"I got a great space," he tells me, his face red with pride, "a real beaut, right up front."

We follow a paved pathway that cuts through the woods, and though I know how near the house is, it cannot be seen until we turn a sharp corner and find ourselves at the foot of the waterfall, looking up at Fallingwater.

"I wish I could see it more clearly," says my father.

"It's interesting, Mr. Donovan," Vincent tells him, "not unlike those contemporary homes they're building in Gaithersburg. Personally, I prefer a more traditional style."

Today's guide is younger than the handsome woman Mark and I had. She seems nervous as she tells Vincent that he cannot bring his drink inside, twenty people waiting as he chugs his chocolate milk before the tour can begin.

"Welcome to Fallingwater," she reads from a piece of paper, her voice as pale as her skin. "My name is Penny."

We start in the living room, Penny reading us some of the house's highlights, using her hands to indicate different sections of the room, like a flight attendant reviewing safety procedures.

"Underneath the floor is the waterfall," reads Penny, "and if you look out the window behind me, you will see the perpendicular beams that hold the house in balance."

Penny is pointing to the wrong window and it makes me sad. If Mark were here, he'd correct her, directing the group's attention to the proper window and calling the beams by their proper name, cantilevers. I say nothing; the others in the group don't know what they're looking for, merely enjoying the view of the forest, then following Penny to the dining area, but my mother stays behind.

"I don't see it," she says, kneeling on a sofa for a closer look, her face pressed against the window, steaming the glass as she speaks.

"No one is allowed on the furniture," Penny says timidly, the entire group turning toward my mother.

"I don't see anything holding this house up," my mother says loudly, now sitting on the sofa, her arms crossed as she leans back, misjudging the height of the cushion and hitting her head on the stone wall.

"Marge," my father says, "this is the limit. This really is the limit."

"She can't sit there," says Penny.

"Time to get up, Mom," Katie says. "Rest hour's over."

"Please don't make me call security," Penny tries.

"But my head hurts from that damn wall," says my mother, and someone in the group starts to laugh.

"Let's get out of here," my father says.

"I told you we should have left her at the hotel," says Vincent. "Mrs. Donovan's not herself today."

"You go on with the tour," I tell them. "I've already seen the house. I'll wait here with Mom."

"But she can't sit there," whines Penny.

"I know, Penny," I say, and when I ask my mother to get up, she does. Penny leads the tour upstairs to the bedrooms and I take my mother to the foyer, where there are chairs we can sit on. She holds my hand, and I can tell by her slightly loosened grip that she's starting to sober up.

"I embarrassed you," she says.

"You didn't," I tell her. "That guide was no good."

"Neither am I," says my mother.

"What are you talking about?"

"Freddy, I'm a bad mother."

"No," I say, remembering the few times I agreed and begged her to stop drinking. Her initial response was always silence, followed by screams of suicide, a blocked attempt to hurl herself off the second-story deck, and, once, a slit wrist.

"I'm bad," she repeats, her voice getting weepy. "Your father and I drove over a bridge on our way here this morning, and for an instant I thought about driving off it. Right through the railing, into the water."

"I'm glad you didn't," I say softly.

"Why?" she asks. "What have I got to live for?"

She's asked me this before. I never know the answer. It occurs to me that Mark will die before she does. It occurs to me that I might die before she does, too. I become aware of water rushing underneath the house, and though I am squeezing my mother's hand as hard as I can, she doesn't seem to feel it.

■ ■ ■ ■

I drive on the way home from Fallingwater. Vincent sits next to me, reviewing the free brochure Penny distributed.

"Good choice," he says, as if I'd chosen it. "I'm glad I got to see Fallingwater, though I was expecting to be more impressed."

I concentrate on the road, pressing the accelerator to give me some power for the steep hill we're about to climb.

"It's not a place I'd want to live in," my father agrees. I see his face in the rearview mirror, his eyes dazed and open wide, as though he just woke up from a long nap.

"I may not be an architect...," says Vincent.

"No," I say, "you're not."

"But I am a homeowner," he says, "and your sister and I house-hunted for months before we bought, so I'm pretty good at sizing a place up."

We are nearing the peak of the hill so I downshift for more pickup.

"Freddy, please," says Katie.

"What?" I ask.

"Slow down," she says.

"The house has great historical value, but, Freddy," Vincent tells me, "you must admit it's loaded with flaws. Small kitchen, small master bedroom, limited garage space..."

"Shut up," I tell him, giving the car enough gas to get us to the top, watching the speedometer climb.

"I'm entitled to my opinion," says Vincent, "and frankly, I wouldn't want to pay the heating bill for that place."

"Shut up," I say, pressing my foot against the gas pedal as we round the hill and head back down again.

"That's no way to speak to your brother-in-law," says my father, a lawyer making a courtroom objection.

Vincent continues, "Admit it, Freddy, it's an impractical, outdated—"

"SHUT UP," I shout, those two words stuck in my throat, repeated over and over again as I floor the accelerator and send the car racing down the hill. My sister screams, but I'm screaming louder, pressing the horn as hard as I'm pressing the gas pedal, the car wailing while I scream, "Shut up shut up shut up shut up shut up," until unshed tears replace the words, choking me so I can no longer make sound. I lift my foot from the pedal, my hand from the horn as we reach the bottom, coasting halfway up the next hill and into a deserted gas station with rusty pumps.

"That was a damn fool thing to do," says my father.

"You could have killed us," Vincent says, his face white, his shirt drenched in sweat.

"You're lucky there wasn't a policeman waiting at the bottom of that hill," my father tells me. "Breaking the speed limit, reckless driving. You'd pay a mighty stiff—"

"Shut up."

But I am not speaking, not yet able to speak. I hear a slight drawl on the "up," and know it's my mother's voice.

"You had it coming," she tells Vincent.

I turn around and look at her. Tears are rolling down her wrinkled face, dripping onto her dirty blouse.

"So did you," I tell her. "You all had it coming."

She grabs my hand and kisses it, holding it against her cheek while she sobs, shaking her head as if answering no to some unspoken question. We sit for minutes under the shade of overgrown trees, next to abandoned pumps. Finally my father speaks.

"Vincent, perhaps you should drive."

Vincent opens his door and comes around to the driver's side. I expect him to gloat as I hand him the keys, but he seems sad, perhaps sorry, and concerned for my sister, who's still trembling with fear. Katie moves up front with Vincent. He kisses her on the forehead before starting the car, the first time I've seen them kiss since their wedding.

I get in back next to my mother. My father is leaning out his open window, looking for oncoming cars as if he can see, while Vincent pulls cautiously onto the road, using his turn signal. I lay my head on my mother's shoulder and she runs her fingers through my hair, lulling my eyes shut with hushed words and gentle sighs. Vincent drives at an even pace, a manual version of cruise control, and soon, all I feel is my mother's hand, all I hear is my mother's heartbeat. My head rises and falls to the rhythm of her breath, and though I can tell by her breathing that she is no longer crying, I can tell by my breathing that I am.

L'ATTRAPE DE COEUR

Italy is hotter than they had expected it to be in September, and despite the air-conditioning of their luxury hotels and the spend, spend, spend feeling that inspired this vacation, they are both uncomfortable. Freddy had hoped that the hills of Tuscany, the ruins of Rome would be romantic, but the heat wave is making Mark feel sicker and Freddy restless, and even the Venetian moon can't make Mark forget that they are the only same-sex couple at every hotel they check into, every restaurant they eat at.

"I feel so conspicuous," Mark says on their first night in Venice, after Freddy has convinced him to go on a gondola ride around the lagoon. "Two gays in a gondola."

"Sounds like the beginning of a joke," says Freddy, but Mark does not laugh, and at breakfast the next morning, Freddy suggests they go to Paris.

They work together to get there, Freddy packing, Mark making travel arrangements. A porter arrives to lead them to the water taxi several blocks away, but he barely has room for their bags, his dolly already piled high with Louis Vuitton luggage, trunks, and garment bags that belong to another gay couple, the first Freddy and Mark have seen in Italy. To Freddy, the men

Dick Scanlan

look more like twins than lovers, in their sixties and almost identical, each carrying a monogrammed cosmetics case, and Freddy wonders whether he and Mark would one day look alike if they grew old together. Neither man says anything to Freddy and Mark, or to each other, their dainty shoes clicking against the old Venetian streets as they jog to keep up with their luggage. The porter pushes the dolly like a tank through narrow alleys, over arched bridges, and Freddy laughs at the sight, startled tourists and angry Italians leaping out of the way as four fags and their trousseau charge past them. Mark too is smiling, and though his face is flushed, his shirt stained with sweat when they finally reach the water taxi, he looks less frail to Freddy than he has in the last month.

■ ■ ■ ■

Their hotel sits at the end of a tiny street on the Left Bank, guarded by a gateway, set back by a courtyard. It wasn't easy to find, their cabdriver clearly having never heard of the hotel or the street. Mark argued with the cabdriver in French as Freddy argued with Mark in English, convinced every turn was a wrong one.

"I studied the French language and French architecture in college," Mark told Freddy, "not the street plan of Paris."

It doesn't have a view. When Freddy pulls back the floor-to-ceiling drapes that hang in their room, he sees a stone wall six inches from their window. This kind of hotel offers the luxury of privacy, the carpets thick, the walls draped with flowered fabric, cushioning the sound. Freddy continues his inspection of the room, opening the desk drawer and feeling the flimsy stationery. He finds a brochure, which he reads aloud to Mark through the closed bathroom door.

"'Built in the fifteenth century, this former monastery has been converted into one of the most exclusive hotels in Paris.' I doubt that," says Freddy, "but at least they gave us a double bed."

"What would the monks say?" asks Mark.

"Are you kidding? The monks would be thrilled." They haven't slept in the same bed since leaving New York, their check-ins at every Italian hotel and pensione delayed as the housekeeping staff hurriedly made up single beds when they saw that their reservation was for two men. The beds were usually placed at the farthest points in the room, like a college dorm, the mattresses more like army cots, narrow and six feet long. Mark slept soundly, but Freddy lay awake, wishing he wasn't alone, his toes dangling two inches off the edge of the bed.

It is almost nine when they step outside their hotel to find a place for dinner. There is a restaurant a few doors down where Mark wants to eat, tired from today's traveling, but Freddy is skeptical since the restaurant's not listed in his gourmet guide to Paris. He is looking up the name, l'Attrape de Coeur, in his French-English dictionary, as if that will shed some light on the quality of the food, when a man, not much older than Freddy but significantly shorter and mustached, opens the door and speaks to them in French. "Bon soir" is all Freddy can make out, so he waits for Mark to translate.

"He's the owner," Mark tells him. "He's inviting us inside, offering to buy us a drink." Mark and the man are both looking to Freddy for an answer, and when he nods yes, the man seems delighted, leading them through the dark green dining room to a table in the back. Freddy runs his hand along the pale yellow tablecloth, places the thick napkin on his lap, smells the white roses. Mark looks less pale by candlelight, his blue eyes aglow, and Freddy is glad they came here.

"Did you figure out what it means, l'Attrape de Coeur?" asks Mark.

"I think it's 'to catch or capture the heart.'"

"Well, you certainly did that to the owner."

Freddy smiles. "Business must be off," he says, but he knows Mark is right. He also knows Mark likes it when men look at Freddy, blond and tan and especially tall in Paris, which tonight gets them a free bottle of wine. Freddy finishes it himself since

Mark is supposed to stay away from alcohol, so they are both woozy on the short walk back to the hotel, Mark from exhaustion and Freddy from the wine.

Their bed has been turned back, chocolates in gold foil left on each of their pillows. Freddy undresses quickly and gets into bed, eating both chocolates. The sheets feel cool on his skin, and he waits for the warmth of Mark's body pressing against his. Mark turns off the light, leaving the room so dark that Freddy can't see, but Mark holds him close enough for Freddy to feel how Mark's body has changed even since they left New York: sharp ribs that poke, bony arms that jab.

▪ ▪ ▪ ▪

Freddy's up early writing postcards. He travels with a mailing list detailing who gets one card per trip (actors he's worked with), one card per city (family, his and Mark's), and one card per day (his closest friends). He calculates that by the end of the two weeks he will have mailed over ninety postcards, and this pleases him, though he quotes that figure to Mark as if the postcard project is a chore.

"What could there possibly be to say?" asks Mark. "You just mailed a stack yesterday from Venice."

"Much has happened," Freddy tells him.

"Really? Then you must have slipped out while I was sleeping."

Freddy finishes today's pile of cards and hands them to Mark, who reads each one, sometimes adding his name at the bottom. When they leave the room Mark is carrying the cards as he does all their important papers: passports, airline tickets, travelers' checks. Freddy has their guidebooks and a map, which he's already unfolded, planning their day with the concierge. This is the first picture Mark takes in Paris, Freddy, sunglasses on, guidebooks open, map spread out on the front desk. Mark has scrapbooks full of Freddy, six years of photos. He's bought as many cameras as they've taken trips, shooting Freddy underwater with a Hanimex, onstage with a long-distance lens, in bed with a

Polaroid. Sometimes they stop a stranger or use the timer to take one together, but Mark looks nervous next to Freddy, who's comfortable in front of a camera.

They head toward the Seine. It is a clear sunny day, and when they reach the bridge they see sunbathers on the concrete banks of the river below, sprawled out on large towels, barely clad in brightly colored bathing suits. Mark is ready to take a picture of these Parisians, but Freddy sees something else that interests him, and he points across the river.

"I know, the Louvre," says Mark. "I told you it was close."

"No," Freddy tells him. "Just beyond it." He gestures to the Tuilleries, once Marie Antoinette's private garden. The trees are in full bloom, their lushness making them no less symmetrical, perfectly straight rows of light brown bark topped in vivid green, like the Rockettes wearing elaborate headdresses. Rising above the trees, Freddy has spotted a Ferris wheel. It looks low-tech, lit in neon and moving slowly, like a 1950s Ferris wheel, and Freddy reorganizes their itinerary to first fit in a ride.

"I don't understand why someone who's afraid of heights would want to ride a Ferris wheel," Mark says.

"Anything that moves," says Freddy. "Ferris wheels, ski lifts, the Coney Island roller coaster. What I can't handle is climbing to the top of a tall building and looking down."

They cross the Pont du Carrousel, which, according to Mark, refers to a monument and not a merry-go-round, and find an amusement park set up at the edge of the gardens, bordering the rue de Rivoli. Directly across the street are some of Paris's finest restaurants and boutiques, but they seem miles away amidst the blinking lights, tinny music, and games that no one is playing, from water guns to weight guessing. Each game promises prizes that are "magnifique," though the dusty shelves of stuffed animals hardly look worth winning.

"I feel like I'm at the county fair," Freddy says.

"For an unusually small county," adds Mark. "The fair's only three blocks long."

Freddy stops at a concession stand and buys two crêpes, but Mark is not hungry so Freddy finishes them both as they stroll along the narrow strip, stopping at every ride: the carousel, the bumper cars, the teacups that go round and round.

"They should be demitasse," says Freddy.

"I still wouldn't ride them," Mark says. "I'm not going near a ride that makes me feel sick to my stomach. I feel that way enough of the time."

"Do you feel okay now?" Freddy asks him.

"Define 'okay.'"

"Maybe we should go back to the hotel," says Freddy.

"No." Mark smiles. "I want to ride the Ferris wheel with you."

"You're having a Coke first," Freddy tells him, returning to the concession stand. "Good for an upset stomach."

Freddy is up on his home remedies, what gets fed and what gets starved, but there is no remedy for AIDS, which is why the doctors don't use the word, a death knell of a diagnosis, focusing instead on the ailment of the day, from diarrhea to pneumonia. Mark reports each new symptom as if he's a war correspondent bringing Freddy news from the front, and though Freddy cheers him on, Freddy views the virus as enemy troops occupying his life. He imagines the swastikas that hung throughout Paris during World War II, and longs for the liberation.

No one is riding the Ferris wheel, but the bored-looking barker doesn't seem to notice and he keeps it running, empty car after empty car floating past Freddy, who, together with Mark, makes up the entire ticket holders' line. The barker reminds Freddy of a drunken sailor, disheveled and vaguely threatening. He keeps his filthy hands over his mouth, holding his cigarette in place until it burns so far down the hot ash touches his fingers. He flicks it over their heads, pulls another from the pack pinned under his brass belt buckle, and yanks on a long lever to stop the ride.

The cars are large enough for six people, two benches facing each other, like some of the trains they took in Italy. They each stretch out on their own bench, Mark's camera ready to go as the car slowly rises up, soaring past the trees of the Tuilleries to give them a panoramic view of Paris. Freddy feels like he is flying and it makes him laugh as Mark takes pictures of Freddy with Paris far below in the background. Together they find the sights of the city, starting with the most famous (the Eiffel Tower, the Opera, Montmarte) and working their way down to their hotel and last night's restaurant. The ride goes on long after they've exhausted their knowledge of Parisian points of interest, the barker directly under them smoking cigarette after cigarette, but neither of them minds, for the motion is constant enough for Freddy, slow enough for Mark. Mark closes his eyes, the breeze blowing through his brown hair, and behind him, Freddy can see couples strolling along the Seine, skinny men and skinny women with their hands in each other's back pocket.

■ ■ ■ ■

One of the artists is staring at Freddy from the other end of the open-air market. Freddy feels the man's eyes following him as he and Mark make their way through the crowd, stopping to look at his watercolors with bold strokes and muted pastels. His subject matter is the same as the other artists' they've seen this afternoon, paintings of Paris and portraits of tourists, but his work is better. Freddy smiles at him and the man responds in French.

"He wants to paint you," Marks tells Freddy.

"How much?" asks Freddy.

This much English the artist understands. He answers to Mark, since it is obvious that Freddy doesn't know French, using his hands while he speaks. Freddy notices his forearms, tanned and splattered with paint. His fingers are stained in beautiful shades, and Freddy sees no brushes on his easel.

"He'll do it for free," says Mark, "and if we like it, we buy it."

Mark puts new film in his camera as the painter prepares a clean piece of paper and arranges his paints. Already a crowd is forming, artists from nearby stalls and tourists looking for something to see. Their eyes dart back and forth between Freddy and the canvas, but the artist's gaze is steady, his eyes bluer than any of his paints.

There is a rhythm to the way this artist works, tentatively at first, as if he's waiting to see how the painting will respond to his touch. He never smiles, though Freddy thinks he must be pleased with what he's doing because he begins to work faster, rubbing his finger in the red, dabbing it in the white. His long hair falls in his face and he pushes it back, streaking it pink. Now he is mixing paints on his fingers without even looking, like a pianist always hitting the right keys. Mark stands directly behind him, one eye open and pressed against the camera, but the painter does not seem distracted by the constant clicking of the shutter.

Freddy can tell by the comments of the crowd that the portrait is good. A few people even applaud when it is finished, and for a moment, Freddy feels proud, as if it were something about him that inspired the painter and made the work special. Only Mark seems displeased with the painting, and when the artist shows it to Freddy, Freddy sees that it's not quite right. He studies it, unable to figure out the flaw. The colors are nice, the hairline is good, and the expression seems perfect, eyes open wide, lips barely parted.

"It's the jaw," says Mark. "It's too square, not long enough." The painter does not understand, and Mark doesn't know the French word for 'jaw,' so Mark points to that part of the portrait, then takes Freddy's face in his hands, running his fingers along Freddy's jaw. Still, the man is disappointed and Freddy is tempted to buy it.

"I've got it on film," Mark whispers.

"I don't want to hurt his feelings."

"It's his finances you'll be hurting," says Mark. "That's what he cares about."

Freddy lets Mark lead him away, turning back for one last look before leaving the market. The artist is not at his stall, maybe taking a break or watching another painter work. Sitting on the easel Freddy sees his portrait, staring out at the crowd, waiting to feel the man's fingers touch his face again.

▪ ▪ ▪ ▪

They see the Ferris wheel when they step outside the restaurant, a cellar wine bar on the Ile de la Cité used as a hiding place by Jews during the War. There are lights along the spokes of the wheel that were impossible to see in the sun, casting a pink glow on the trees below. It is almost midnight, and Mark surprises Freddy by suggesting they go for a ride.

"You're not tired?" Freddy asks.

"A little," says Mark, "but I'm up for a late-night spin."

This time there is a short line, mostly male-female couples who stare at Freddy's and Mark's dark blazers and silk ties, appropriate for tonight's restaurant but too formal for a Ferris wheel. The barker doesn't seem to notice their clothes as he helps them into a car, and Freddy wonders if he remembers them from this morning.

As soon as their car has risen past the trees they move close together, sharing the same bench and holding hands. Paris is illuminated, spotlights shining on its best-known buildings, twinkling bulbs the color of Christmas tree lights lining the tops of the tents below. The night air is cool, and Freddy puts his arm around Mark, keeping it there as the car comes back around, passing the barker and heading up into the dark sky. They are at the tallest point when the Ferris wheel stops, hanging high over the City like a star.

"Are you okay?" Mark asks.

Freddy feels lightheaded, the way a child can turn and turn, but not get dizzy until he stops.

"I'll be fine," he tells Mark, "as long as I don't look directly down."

"There's not much to see down there, but you can look. I won't let you fall."

"It's more a fear of being pulled down, like by a magnet," Freddy explains. "When I was a kid I couldn't get near a body of water without ending up all wet. Pools, creeks, lakes, I'd stand on the edge, looking at my reflection, and the next thing I knew I'd be swimming."

"You're safe from the Seine up here," says Mark, "unless you can fly."

They gaze out at the white lights reflected on the water, shining on the banks of the river, which are busy tonight with men taking solitary walks. Their pace is slow, but it seems purposeful, like a chess game: a man moves from the bench where he's sitting, causing another to stop and light a cigarette. Heads turn as men pass each other, but they keep walking, constantly reversing directions so they pass each other again. It looks almost choreographed, but Freddy notices a spot where the dancers disappear, under the Pont du Carrousel. One by one they're swallowed by the shadow of the bridge overhead, hidden from view even from Freddy's vantage point.

Their car jolts forward when the Ferris wheel starts, dropping several feet, and Freddy panics. There is no seatbelt, no safety bar to strap him in, but Mark has Freddy pinned to the bench as if he too is afraid that Freddy will be launched into the night, soaring toward the Seine like a programmed missile. The wheel continues to stop and start, unloading the passengers car by car, and though Freddy gets used to these sudden drops, his legs are still shaky when they finally reach the ground.

Again they get a cabdriver who's unfamiliar with the former monastery. Mark tries to direct him, but the driver stops a few blocks away from their hotel, giving them an explanation in French.

"He's saying something about one-way streets and no left turns," Mark tells Freddy. "We can walk from here."

They walk along the boulevard St. Germain, lined with street vendors and crowded cafes even at this late hour, but the tiny street leading to their hotel is quiet and dark, as if there's still a monastery at the end of the block. The only light is coming from l'Attrape de Coeur, though it is closed, the tables stacked inside, the waiters no longer wearing uniforms as they sit at the bar, having a drink with the owner. He spots Freddy and Mark, stepping outside to greet them.

"How are you enjoying Paris?" he asks, his accent thick but his English perfect.

Freddy answers, the first time he's been able to do so today without filtering his response through Mark's French.

"It's a beautiful city," he says.

"And the Parisians? Are we living up to our reputation?"

"I've had no problems," Freddy tells him, "but we're from New York City. It makes me nervous if someone is too nice."

"Well, I do not wish to make you nervous," says the man, "but I hope you return to l'Attrape de Coeur. We will toast your next trip to Paris."

"It's an interesting name for a restaurant," Mark says. "The trap of the heart."

"Literally, yes. But it is an expression," the man explains, searching for the words in English. "If someplace is l'Attrape de Coeur, it sucks you in even though it may be bad for you. It is a place you cannot resist going, because it feels so good."

"Or tastes so good," says Mark, "like your restaurant."

The owner bids them bon soir, and they continue walking. Halfway to their hotel, the street turns suddenly darker. Freddy glances back and sees that the lights of l'Attrape de Coeur have been shut off.

The gate that guards the hotel is locked.

"I hope the monks are still awake," Mark says, ringing the bell. Freddy watches through the wrought-iron bars as the concierge crosses the empty courtyard to let them in.

They leave the night-light on when they get into bed, glowing dimly, like a candle. This time Mark eats his chocolate, unwrapping the other and feeding it to Freddy, then kissing him good night, their lips sealed shut for reasons of safety, like a stage kiss. Freddy closes his eyes and Mark's fingers trace the shape of his lips as if he's fingerpainting them, trying to draw the perfect portrait.

■ ■ ■ ■

It takes Freddy three museums to find what he is looking for. He combs each gift shop, list in hand, choosing postcards as carefully as Christmas presents. He buys a different Degas for each of his dancer friends, pictures of the Louvre for his family, and the Mona Lisa for Mark's. At the Musée Picasso he sees a painting of women sunbathing on a rocky beach, their bodies elongated, their hands fixing their hair. This is the card he will send his best friends, writing something about his and Mark's new hairdos and the bikinis they bought in Paris. Freddy's sure that friends will notice Mark's weight loss when they return to New York, but he'll hold off telling them until they ask, comforted by these postcard-length conversations in which Mark is still healthy and Freddy is not afraid.

He finishes the cards, counting today's stack, then tallying the total amount he's spent on postcards and stamps this trip. He adds a hundred thousand lira to two hundred francs and comes up with a figure well over a hundred dollars. He wants to tell Mark, but Mark is napping, tired from the museums. Freddy watches him dream, wondering whether he sees a happy future or only the past. Freddy knows that Mark has nightmares, his body so drenched in sweat that he has to shower as Freddy changes the sheets. The doctors say that sweat is safe, but the virus has been found in tears, and sometimes Freddy is frightened when Mark weeps, holding Mark's hand yet keeping his distance.

The postcards are ready to go, and though Freddy realizes that he and Mark will get to New York before the cards do, he wants to mail them from here. He writes Mark a note on a spare Picasso, leaving the hotel with no map or guidebook, since he knows there's a mailbox across from l'Attrape de Coeur. Freddy looks for the owner, but sees only the staff inside. A few of the waiters seem to recognize him, and he waves after he drops the cards into the box, the first time he's had his hands free in France. He puts them in his pockets, which are empty, his money on the dresser back at the room.

Freddy didn't know how noisy this tiny street could get, bustling with workers on their way home. He sees two women, chic and sophisticated and sharing an order of McDonald's french fries. That is a picture Mark would take, but Freddy is glad that there's no camera, no one watching him as he walks past the cloistered silence of the monastery and into rush-hour Paris.

There are crowds at every movie theater and outdoor cafe. The stores are so full their doors are open, the smell of fresh bread stopping Freddy as he passes a bakery, but he has no cash for even the smallest treat. He stands outside the bakery, the heat of the ovens and the afternoon sun making him thirsty, so he crosses the bridge, heading for the shade of the Tuilleries Gardens.

Even the amusement park is busy, people actually playing the games. There are long lines at every ride, the longest by far for the Ferris wheel. The barker seems unimpressed that his is the main attraction, probably resenting the extra work, able to smoke only one cigarette before he must stop the wheel and let the next load of passengers on. His shadow has become a beard, as if he's been there all night, and he's wearing the same clothes as yesterday, his belt tightened a notch, the buckle crushing his almost empty pack of cigarettes. Freddy wonders if he could convince the barker to let him ride without any money to pay his fare. He'd have to find a way to ask, for he's sure the barker speaks as little English as he does French, maybe pulling his pockets inside out and pointing to an empty car.

From high above, Freddy hears squeals, and he sees that the Ferris wheel has stopped, leaving somebody stranded as he was last night. These screams are playful, almost flirtatious, schoolgirls trying to get the barker's attention, but the barker doesn't look up. Freddy's screams would be real if he were stuck up there without Mark, though maybe he'd be too terrified to make a sound, knowing that the barker below would ignore his cries.

The barker throws back the lever that starts the wheel, the squeals becoming giggles that blend in with the tinkling music.

Freddy can still hear them when he leaves the fair, walking through the Tuilleries. He sees a circle of men sitting in ice cream parlor chairs, watching the wading pool in the center where a tiny boat is floating. They are serious and silent, as if controlling the boat by communal thought, but Freddy knows that one of them must have a remote, for the boat makes sharp turns and sudden stops despite the calm current of the water.

Again Freddy thinks of Mark and his camera, the scenes of Paris he's missing today, the gap in the scrapbook between this afternoon's museums and this evening's late dinner. Each scrapbook is titled, the photos inside labeled like the center section of a star's biography. Freddy is the fifth child of parents who couldn't figure out how to work a camera. By the time he came along they'd grown tired of trying, so there's one photo of Freddy at four, another on his twelfth birthday, and not much more until he met Mark. He remembers his Baby Book, bought when he was born almost thirty years ago and still blank, and he worries that Mark will leave him with a half-finished photo album, a half-dozen cameras, and no one to take his picture.

Now he is watching a real boat, a sight-seeing barge on the Seine, wondering how it will fit under the low bridge he's standing on. The top deck is filled with tourists who Freddy can almost touch as they pass under the bridge. A few of them wave and he waves back, holding his hand up until the boat is gone and Freddy can see his shadow on the river below, swirling on the water in the wake of the boat. For a moment he is dizzy, as though his shadow is accurate, mirroring him as he loses his balance. He steadies himself on the stone wall, looking for someplace to sit, and spots the benches on the banks of the river.

The steps are narrow and steep, almost like a ladder, leading directly down to the path along the Seine, which is lined with bushes that seem to rustle when Freddy walks by. Several of the benches are taken by men sitting alone, and though there is room for Freddy, he heads in the direction of his hotel, not sitting until he finds an empty bench. He looks back at the bridge he's crossed.

Freddy doesn't know what it's called, memorizing where it is so he and Mark can locate it later on the map. The benches he passed are now vacant, though the path is deserted, and Freddy wonders where the men have gone.

There is movement in the bushes behind him. The hedges are high, woven together densely enough to hide in, but Freddy glimpses a patch of denim through an opening left by a broken branch. He can tell when it moves that it is someone's leg, though he doesn't know which part. Freddy stands up and starts walking, approaching the Pont du Carrousel. A man is leaning against the base of the stone bridge, and though Freddy can't see into the darkness under the bridge, he looks through it and notices a man on the other end. Occasionally one of the two men wanders into the shadows cast by the bridge above, but they reappear, posted like sentries on either side of the underpass.

Freddy feels this side's sentry staring at him, and others too, watching him from behind the bushes, under the bridge, their eyes accustomed to the dark. The sentry says something in French and Freddy stops at the foot of the steps that would take him to the street above, close enough to the sentry to smell his cigarette, foreign and strong. Again the man speaks, this time gesturing to the path under the Pont du Carrousel. Freddy walks to the edge of the underpass, where the early evening light stops, reminded of a theatre game in which two actors are separated by a stick on the floor, each trying different tactics to lure the other onto his side: seduction, intimidation, manipulation, whatever it takes to win.

Someone whispers from the darkness. Freddy can see lit cigarettes but not the hands that hold them, and he realizes how many men are waiting for him on the other side of the stick. Mark is probably awake by now, waiting for Freddy at the hotel a half block away, but Freddy feels no pull in that direction. Instead, he steps over the line, yet he feels as if he's won the game, going someplace where he has a future and leaving Mark behind. Bodies brush against Freddy's, but no hands grab him, no fingers touch his skin, and it is impossible to make out faces. He leans against one of the bridge's cement supports, rough as sandpaper, rising diagonally over the river like the upright boards movie stars lounge on when they don't want to wrinkle their costume. He lies in the dark, his skin sticking through his clothes to the cold concrete, the way flesh sticks to ice.

Freddy wonders what another man will feel like, but all he comes up with is what he knew before Mark got sick, remembering the pictures of him and Mark having sex. He wants to burn those pictures, shred them, cut them in half and fill Mark's place with the owner of l'Attrape de Coeur. He imagines them drunk with champagne, making love in the monastery. The owner is trying to please Freddy, but Freddy is nothing more than tickled by his mustache, so instead, Freddy feels the artist's fingers on his skin, using his body as a canvas. Freddy tries to hold the position the artist wants to paint him in, his muscles burning, cramping, trembling until finally he collapses and the painting is ruined.

The sound of a match being struck brings Freddy back under the bridge. An orange glow flashes on a man's face as he lights a cigarette. The man disappears when he blows out the match, but Freddy holds onto his face, making his hair darker, giving him a beard, turning him into the barker. Freddy shivers in the cool dampness, his head spinning as he closes his eyes and pictures kissing the barker. Even in his fantasy, the barker doesn't respond, but Freddy keeps going, fueled only by his own desire, sinking to his knees and begging the barker to keep the wheel turning as Freddy unbuckles the barker's belt.

Matinee

Lizzie is seated seventh row center watching me play croquet and sing.

"The sun has got his hat on, hip-hip-hip-hooray..."

I like being watched, her gaze following me upstage and out of the light as I freeze for the star's tap solo. Lizzie has seen me on television but never onstage, though she boasts to her classmates about her famous Uncle Freddy, compiling my TV appearances onto a single videotape as a show-and-tell project, plenty of room for future clips.

"Now we'll all be happy, hip-hip-hip-hooray..."

Mark tries to watch me, barely strong enough to keep his head afloat in the sea of white- and blue- and pink-haired matinee ladies. As the dance break builds, the ensemble joins the star, and Mark's eyes are on my feet. He knows I hadn't tapped until this show cast me in the chorus, hiding me in back during big dance numbers, and though it might look like I'm keeping up with the intricate footwork, I'm merely air tapping, moving my feet in the right direction without making a sound, my tap shoe never touching the floor.

"The sun has got his hat on and he's coming out today!"

Dick Scanlan

Big smile, big finish, hold for applause. Lizzie is on her feet, cheering, "Bravo!" the way I told her to, until Granny P. leans over, saying something that makes Lizzie sit down and stop cheering.

P is for Patricia, but we all call her Granny: Lizzie, me, my parents, though she is no relation to any of us. She came with my brother's new wife, part of the package, instant grandmother to Lizzie, my brother's child from a previous marriage. Granny P. has been sent along as a chaperone, sitting between Lizzie and Mark, looking up at the lights, down at the pit, then at two old ladies in the next aisle who were talking until Granny P. silenced them with her glare, as if she's responsible for the audience's behavior, not just Lizzie's.

The orchestra starts the play-off and the chorus goes tapping into the wings, out of sight of the audience. We tiptoe downstairs to our dressing room under the stage: we don't want the click-clacking of our tap shoes to disrupt the scene between the young lovers above us. There are five and five, men and women, sharing one long table, each of us looking in the lighted mirror, touching up our makeup.

Dressing room chatter.

Boy #1: Who has a screwdriver?

Girl #1: Isn't it a bit early in the day?

Boy #1: The tool, not the cocktail, to tighten my tap.

Girl #2: Try taking class.

Boy #2: It hasn't helped your dancing.

Girl #3: That stage is too slippery to dance on.

Boy #3: I nearly fell.

Girl #4: This crowd wouldn't have noticed.

T.J. talks to my reflection in the mirror, dusting his caramel-colored face with what looks like cocoa powder.

"Freddy, your niece is a doll. Jean Harlow at eight."

"She's blonde and blue-eyed," I say. "I don't know about Harlow. How'd you spot her?"

"Easy," says T.J. "She's the only person out there under ninety."

Everyone laughs and I think of Mark, his features sunken, his skin gray, his eyes still an elfin blue, like an old man who's young at heart, rather than a young man who's ill.

"Lizzie wants to meet all of you after the show," I say, addressing the length of the mirror, "and she wants two autographed programs, one for her and one for her best friend Laura. Apparently it's Laura's birthday next week."

"The big zero-nine," T.J. says.

"And your niece is giving her a *Playbill?*" asks Veronica, who looks old for the chorus but young for her age. "Cheap."

"Not like her uncle," says T.J., blowing me a kiss in the mirror.

"Since the divorce she spends alternate weekends in Baltimore," I tell Veronica. "What can I say?"

I leave my makeup on after the show, doing a quick change into my own clothes, accustomed to rushing home and bringing Mark a meal, giving him his medication before hurrying back to the theatre for the evening performance. At first I felt conspicuous wearing makeup outside the theatre: it's considered unprofessional, though I don't use much and this is New York City, where no one pays attention to a little mascara on a man.

Lizzie does, making me close my eyes so she can study my darkened lashes. She's ready for a tour of the set, but Mark and Granny P. remain in their seats as if the play is still in progress. They look more like a couple than Mark and I do, the thin layer of colorless, postchemotherapy fuzz coating Mark's scalp hardly out of place next to Granny P.'s gray curls, and although I introduce Lizzie to T.J. and Veronica, I say nothing about the seemingly elderly couple sitting in the empty theatre. I've told Mark all about T.J. and Veronica, but I've not told anyone in the cast about Mark. I like having a place to come every day where nobody knows my boyfriend is dying of AIDS. They don't even know I have a boyfriend.

"Why wasn't your part bigger?" Lizzie asks upon seeing the star's dressing room.

"Child," laughs T.J., pure Pearl Bailey, "that's what your uncle's been asking since the first day of rehearsal."

We finish center stage, surrounded by the chorus. They sign Lizzie's programs, Veronica inscribing Laura's with a surprisingly sweet birthday message. Lizzie is going through the cast list, making sure she got everyone's signature, as the actors discuss where to eat between shows: Chinese? Salad bar? Sushi bar?

"How about a *bar* bar," says Veronica, lighting a long cigarette with a gold lighter.

"Can we go with them, Uncle Freddy?" asks Lizzie.

"We're booked for a banana spilt," I remind her.

The other actors leave through the stage door, but we exit through the darkened theatre, stopping at row G to pick up Mark and Granny P. Lizzie skips ahead to the lobby as I help Mark up the aisle, and by the time we step outside, Lizzie's hailed us a taxi, her favorite thing to do in New York. Lizzie, Mark, and Granny P. get in back, and I sit up front with the driver, directing him to the City's most sophisticated ice cream parlor.

"You looked great onstage," says Mark, "like you've been dancing all your life."

"Thanks," I say, but I don't turn around or take my eyes off the road, as if sitting next to the driver somehow involves me in the driving of the cab.

"I loved the costumes," Lizzie says.

"Did you see how neat and clean those costumes were?" asks Granny P. "That's because the actors hang them properly as soon they take them off, like I always tell Lizzie to."

In the rearview mirror, I see Lizzie roll her eyes.

"Actually we have dressers who pick up our costumes for us," I say. "They deserve all the credit."

"I want a dresser," says Lizzie.

"You have one," Granny P. tells her, "with six drawers, but you seem to prefer the floor."

Mark leans forward and instructs the driver to make an initial stop at our apartment.

"No sundae?" I ask him.

"I'm beat," says Mark. "The show wiped me out."

"You have to eat something," I say.

"After my nap, Freddy. Promise."

The taxi pulls up in front of our building, and when the doorman spots Mark, he opens the cab door, offering Mark his uniformed arm. Mark moves slowly, bundled in a baggy gray coat that used to fit him, still feeling the chill of winter though spring's been here for weeks.

"Mark did very well today," reports Granny P. as the cab pulls away. "He even stood up to stretch his legs at intermission. A nice nap and he'll be good as new." Granny P. sounds as if she's discussing a chest cold, and I wonder if her prognosis was made to protect Lizzie from the truth about Mark, or comfort me from the reality of it.

Lizzie likes the ice cream parlor, the pinkest place in town: pink leather banquettes, pink marble floors, and pink old waitresses. We sit at the counter on pink stools, facing a large mirror. Behind us are shelves upon shelves of green rabbits, yellow cats, striped elephants, and Lizzie makes up a game.

"I'll name a shelf," she tells me, "and out of all the stuffed animals in that row, you have to pick out my favorite."

Our food comes, a BLT for me, elaborate sundaes for Granny P. and Lizzie, but Lizzie's more interested in her newly invented game.

"Let Uncle Freddy eat first," says Granny P.

"He can eat and play," Lizzie says. "Third shelf."

I look in the mirror at the reflection of the stuffed animals.

"The panda with the blue bow tie?"

"You guessed it! First shelf."

"Red polka-dotted alligator."

"Two for two, Uncle Freddy. You're good at my game," she says, stirring her uneaten sundae until it becomes soupy.

"Don't play with your food, Lizzie," Granny P. tells her. "You'll never be a debutante if you play with your food."

"What's a debutante?" asks Lizzie.

Granny P. seems unsure of the answer, so I do it for her.

"A rich and beautiful young woman who goes to big balls and rides in limousines."

"I'd rather ride in one of those," Lizzie says, pointing out the window across Fifty-ninth Street to the horse-drawn carriages lined up along Central Park.

"Hansom cabs," I tell her.

"I'll bet they're fun," she says. "Have you and Uncle Mark ever been in a handsome cab?"

Granny P. smiles at me in the mirror.

"No," I say, "we never have."

"Do you and Uncle Mark always sleep in the same bed?" asks Lizzie. Granny P. shakes her head no, feeding me my line.

"Yes, Lizzie. We do." I can tell Granny P. is gritting her teeth beneath her grin, but Lizzie seems satisfied with my answer, no more questions about Mark and me.

The pink waitress hands me the check, probably assuming I'm Lizzie's father and Granny P.'s son. I pay the bill, feeling very much the man in the family, and I think how nice it would be if someone took me out for ice cream. I imagine myself sitting in this pink parlor with Mark, a healthy Mark, playing Lizzie's game with me and buying me the stuffed animal every time I guess right. Or T.J., referring to our waitress as "Miss Thing," making loud jokes about white boys who prefer chocolate as I order my fourth hot-fudge sundae. Even Veronica, smoking a cigarette and savoring a martini while I work on a ten-dollar banana split.

Lizzie plays one more round before we leave.

"Fourth shelf," she says.

"White seal wearing sunglasses."

"Nope," says Lizzie. "Guess again."

I see my face in the mirror as I study the fourth shelf of stuffed animals. My skin looks orange, a rose-colored stripe along each cheekbone, and I realize my makeup is not as subtle as I'd thought.

I don't remove my makeup until after the second show, when I get home from the theatre, the first time in twelve hours I've seen my own skin. Lizzie watches me cover my face with cold cream, scrubbing with soap and water until the white washcloth is stained the color of flesh, smeared with black mascara.

"You looked better with it on, Uncle Freddy," Lizzie says. "Not so pale."

"I like him this way," says Mark.

He is sitting on the sofa eating the sandwich I brought, already dressed for bed in a flannel nightshirt I gave him for Christmas, patterned with little cowboys and Indians fighting a never-ending battle. Granny P. sits next to him, sipping herbal tea as she looks out the window at my glamorous view of Manhattan. Her navy blue nightgown is dotted with tiny white flowers, and it somehow seems to fit with the dark night and bright lights of the City.

"It's getting late for Lizzie," Granny P. tells me.

"It's getting late for me," yawns Mark.

"Uncle Freddy promised we'd watch a movie," says Lizzie.

"I did," I admit. "The movie of her choice."

"This has been a big day for her," says Granny P. "The train trip, the play, the ice cream parlor..."

"We'll get the movie started," I say, whispering to Granny P. "Lizzie won't last long once the lights are out."

Granny P. stands in the bedroom doorway, ready to veto any inappropriate titles as Lizzie looks through our tapes.

"*The Sound of Music*," says Mark when Lizzie makes her selection, "Uncle Freddy's favorite."

"Also one of mine," Granny P. says, sitting on the edge of the bed. Lizzie slides under the covers, bundled between Mark and me in her lavender bunny pajamas, like one of those stuffed animals from the shelves of the ice cream parlor.

"This film was my first field trip in first grade," I tell Lizzie. "I felt like I'd floated out of my row of green uniforms and into the movie. Afterwards, I couldn't believe I was back on a bus with

Sister Therasina, no longer traipsing around the Alps with the Von Trapps."

"Is that when you knew you wanted to be an actor?" she asks.

"I think I always knew that," I say, and I wonder what Lizzie knows about the future.

Granny P. slips out of the room. I am surprised she'd leave Lizzie alone with Mark, me, and the nuns, though she's probably seen *The Sound of Music* many times, and this is her first trip to New York, her first glimpse of the glittering skyline outside my living room window. Mark is sleeping, his breath even and untroubled, as if he'll wake up healthy, and Lizzie drifts in and out of sleep. I put my arm around her shoulder, which feels tiny and delicate, but not frail like Mark's.

Now there is a rainstorm in the movie. The children are frightened, gathering on a bed where Julie Andrews sings to soothe them.

"Raindrops on roses and whiskers on kittens..."

"VCR, remote-control color TV, answering machine," says Lizzie, suddenly awake and taking inventory of my apartment.

"Bright copper kettles and warm woolen mittens..."

"Three telephones, a microwave, CD player..."

"Brown paper packages tied up with strings..."

"Word processor, food processor," Lizzie says, looking up at me through sleepy eyes. "I love you and Mark's apartment, Uncle Freddy. It's so modern."

These are a few of my favorite things.

Lizzie is soon asleep, her body curled around Mark's. I turn out the lamp, listen to my movie, and watch them dream, the light from the TV screen flickering across their faces, both of them basking in its pale blue glow.

TEARS OF TWO

It takes Paul over an hour to drive from his house outside Baltimore to his parents' house outside Washington, but he lies when he gets there.

"Forty-five minutes, door to door," he tells his father, who is uninterested in travel times and traffic patterns, unable to drive since his stroke. His father is busy eating dark cherries, spitting the pits into a china bowl where they land with a *ping,* and though Paul is blinded by the winter sunlight pouring in from three directions, his father is prepared with sunglasses, incognito in his own kitchen.

"Thanks for taking the day off work," says his mother.

"The law business will survive," Paul says.

"I'd drive him myself," she explains, setting a grapefruit half on Paul's plate, "but I can't handle that downtown traffic."

He wonders if what she can't handle is Dodie. His mother always mistook Dodie's blonde hair and blue eyes for beauty, as Paul had in adolescence, yet Dodie was really a plain woman with a good paint job, while his mother needed no makeup to emphasize her emerald eyes, no henna to highlight her flaming hair. When his mother was sober, she spoke fondly of Dodie, but fueled by alcohol, she'd accuse his father of being attracted to "that Scandinavian woman," though he never stayed late at the office,

Dick Scanlan

or took business trips without Paul's mother. Still, Paul remembers waking up to their angry voices, his father drunk, his mother more so and insisting that Dodie be fired, her ultimatum always forgotten the following morning.

"Sad about Dodie," says Paul.

"Isn't it?" his mother asks, pouring herself coffee that looks strong enough to eat through her delicate cup.

"She was a fine secretary," his father tells him.

That's what his father said when he called Paul at home last week. Paul was surprised to hear from him: his father rarely calls him, and never at home, always at the office. Grace, whom Paul married the day his divorce from his first wife became final, says she spoke more with Paul's father when she was Paul's receptionist than she has as Paul's wife. His father kept the conversation short, speaking loudly, as if Baltimore was an overseas call from Washington, telling him about Dodie, the clinical terms, the bleak prognosis.

"How old is she?" Paul asks.

"Dodie?" says his father. "Late fifties, I suppose."

"Young," Paul says. "And it's..."

"Ovarian," answers his mother. "Ovarian cancer. She never married," his mother adds, as though Dodie's cancer is connected to her marital status.

"She's married to her work," his father says in Dodie's defense. "One of the best our firm has."

His father speaks as if he is an active partner, though his involvement in his former law firm is now no more than an annual appearance at the Christmas party. Paul has a less favorable view of the men his father worked with for thirty years: not one of them visited during the many weeks his father was hospitalized. Only Dodie, bringing flowers that she said were from the firm, keeping his father informed of the outcomes of his cases.

"What hospital is she in?" his father asks.

"Georgetown," his mother snaps, rinsing a glass with water so hot the window is steaming.

"Where I convalesced," his father mumbles, rising from the table.

"Where our five children were born," she says softly, resting her hands on Paul's shoulders as his father walks slowly down the hall. "He's asked me what hospital Dodie's in a dozen times daily for the past week," whispers his mother. "Nothing new sticks, only details from long ago."

Paul touches his mother's hands, which are warm from the dishwater. His father has disappeared into his library, closing the door behind him and probably opening the window to smoke a forbidden cigar. Paul always smuggles a few in for his father, and though his mother must smell the tobacco on his breath, she plays along, allowing him some pleasure. He pictures his father hurriedly puffing on the thick cigar, waving the smoke out of an open window and into the wintry air like a teenager, surrounded by thousands of books organized in a system only his father understands. He runs it like a law library: books may be browsed through but not checked out. Paul once took a book back to college with him, and, within days, received an angry letter discussing the definition of ownership, demanding the book's return. His father barely reads now, yet he still knows when a book is missing.

His father comes into the kitchen wearing a black coat that hangs off his shoulders, the sleeves hiding all but his fingertips. Most of his father's clothes have been tailored to keep up with his post-stroke weight loss, but not this voluminous topcoat, and he looks lost and little inside it, like a butler on his day off, wearing his master's old clothes.

"Shouldn't you bring flowers or something?" Paul asks his father, who looks to Paul's mother for the answer.

"Most hospitals don't allow flowers for very sick patients," she says.

"Why?" says Paul.

"Germs," she explains. "Dodie's flowers would probably end up at the nurses' station."

She follows them outside without a coat, hugging herself as Paul opens the passenger's door of his new car. His father lowers himself into the leather seat, staring at the controls on the dashboard as if it is a spaceship and trying to figure out which part of the seatbelt is inserted where.

"If I were the man I used to be, I'd take this mandatory-seatbelt law to court," his father says as Paul reaches over to fasten it for him, "challenge its constitutionality."

"It's common sense," says Paul.

"When did common sense become a legal obligation?" asks his father. "I have the right to make the wrong decision."

"A right you've never exercised," says his mother. "Now don't stay too long and tire poor Dodie out."

"Did you give Paul directions to..."

"Georgetown," his mother reminds him.

"I know the way, Dad. I'm not a tourist," says Paul, though his father's treated him like one since Paul left Washington and his first wife, and his mother reviews the route as if the last time Paul traveled it was for his birth, as if he hadn't driven down from Baltimore every day during his father's stay at the same hospital.

His mother waves good-bye with her white dishtowel as Paul pulls out of their circular driveway. His father is searching the door for a handle, but by the time Paul hits a button and the window slides down, his mother is too far away for his father's failed eyesight. Cold air fills the car as his father blows her a misfired kiss, aimed off to the side, into the woods that border Paul's parents' home.

■ ■ ■ ■

His father takes his sunglasses off outside Dodie's door. His face has been frozen in a startled expression since he looked up from his breakfast one morning and asked Paul's mother who she was, but the stroke has slowly lightened his father's brown eyes, the way spoiled chocolate turns white.

"Do you want me to go in with you?" asks Paul.

"Of course, son. Dodie will enjoy seeing you."

Paul opens the door for his father, following him into the room. His father sits next to Dodie, taking her hands in his, and Paul stands at the foot of the bed.

"Two handsome visitors in one day," she says. "Won't the nurses be jealous?" Her voice is weak, though she always spoke softly, as if sharing a secret.

Dodie has prepared for their visit, thickening her thin lips with pink lipstick, powdering her porcelain skin. Paul sees pale blue when she blinks, as though her eyelids are translucent, and he wonders how sick she looks under her makeup. He knows enough about the effects of chemotherapy to assume her elaborate hairstyle is a wig, sprayed into a golden twist with ringlets dangling like earrings on either side of her broad face.

"Are they treating you well?" his father asks.

She laughs lightly, like a rapid series of bubbles blown on one breath. "The people are lovely but the food is rather tasteless," she says, indicating her I.V.

"You look wonderful," says Paul, "as always."

"You've grown up," says Dodie, "but I saw a recent picture of you in the *Sun*."

"Baltimore's paper," his father says, impugning the *Sun*'s credibility. Paul's tried to explain that he moved there by choice, but his father acts as if Paul's in exile, he and Grace a Washington version of Windsor and Wallis Simpson.

"Dad thinks Baltimore is the urban answer to Purgatory," Paul tells Dodie.

"Not Purgatory," his father corrects him. "Hell."

"Well, Baltimore's big on Paul," she says to his father, "'Ten Top Lawyers under 40.'"

Paul didn't send his father this clip: he's sent several over the past four years, none of which his father acknowledged, though before Paul became what his father refers to as a "Baltimoron," he kept up with Paul's accomplishments, dictating Dodie congratulatory notes that began "Dear Son:" and ended with an illegible scrawl, under which Dodie typed "Dad." His father must have kept Dodie informed of Paul's failures as well, because she sent him a handwritten note when he wasn't accepted at Harvard, praising the essay she'd typed for his application, questioning Harvard's judgment. Paul wonders if his father told Dodie about the divorce: he wouldn't discuss it with Paul even in a legal context, saying, "You've got the wrong man. My firm never handled matrimonial law." Still, Dodie must have heard. The secretaries at Paul's firm knew about his affair with the receptionist long before his first wife found out, which means every legal secretary in Washington knew.

Dodie asks about the rest of the family, and Paul lets his father do the talking, though the answers are awkward at first, his father accustomed to Paul's mother being their spokesperson. Dodie nods her head up and down as his father speaks, her mouth somewhere between a gasp and a smile, as if she's holding her breath, preparing to blow out candles on a birthday cake. His father regains a ghost of his former command, telling Dodie about his grandchildren, forgetting their ages, their names, and, if they were born after his stroke, their existence altogether, but Paul does not correct him.

"I remember when Lizzie was born," Dodie tells Paul.

"My oldest," he says as if he has many, though Lizzie's the only child from his first marriage, the twins from his second barely three months old.

"She was the first grandchild of this cigar fiend," says Dodie, pointing to Paul's father. "Not only did he hand out stogies..."

"Cuban," his father interrupts. "Top of the line."

"But he made us smoke them," continues Dodie. "I was sick the entire day, and the office reeked like a poolroom."

"He made me smoke one when Freddy was born," Paul tells her.

"You were only ten years old," she says.

"I know," laughs Paul. "Lizzie's age."

"Don't tell me Lizzie is ten," Dodie says.

"On her next birthday," says Paul, "and almost five feet tall."

"Sounds like a Donovan," she says. "You all look alike, especially you and your father."

"Poor boy," his father says, and then to Paul, "I'm sorry, son."

"Is it a lawyerly glow?" asks Paul.

"It's your features," Dodie explains. "When you were younger, I thought you took after your mother. You've got her red hair, and that beautiful Irish skin, but your features are your father's. Especially your mouth."

Paul tries to smile, but he is suddenly aware of his mouth, as if it had been numbed by Novocaine that is now wearing off. His lips are tingling, and he wonders if he looks uncomfortable, but Dodie's looking at his father. Paul doesn't know where to look. His eyes shift from Dodie, to his father, to the photo on her night table, an old picture of a young man in a military uniform that Paul recognizes from Dodie's desk at work.

Dodie breaks the silence.

"We miss you at the office, Mr. Donovan," she tells his father. "Those younger partners lack your joie de law."

"I'm afraid I've lost it myself, since my impairment."

"No you haven't," she says, shifting in bed and adjusting her I.V. tube gracefully, the way a jazz singer handles a microphone cord. "You'll never lose it."

His father smiles. "The closest I've come to a courtroom lately is reruns of *Perry Mason.*"

"That's where I learned the ropes," Paul says. "Dad used to make me watch *Perry Mason* and analyze the litigation."

"As preparation for law school?" asks Dodie.

"Preparation for junior high," Paul tells her.

"I was only thinking of your future, son."

"It worked," Dodie giggles.

"You should see him, Dodie," Paul says. "Making objections the D.A. missed, holding Perry in contempt of court."

"My apologies to Mr. Mason," his father says grandly, "but there are many episodes in which I would have won."

Dodie is slightly out of breath from laughter, or from her illness, and she dabs at her eyes with a pink Kleenex.

"It's a good thing you never joined our firm," she tells Paul. "We'd do no work with two Donovans in the office."

That offer was made after Paul negotiated the terms of his father's retirement. His father was a young man when he and a few others founded the firm, and they hadn't planned for sickness and strokes. The partners' proposal would have left his parents with little money, forcing them to sell their beautiful house, but Paul fought hard for his father and won, earning enough of the partners' respect to be asked to fill his father's slot. Paul never told his father about the offer, turning it down to stay in Baltimore with his new firm, his new life.

A young nurse walks by Dodie's open door, carrying an arrangement of pale pink roses wrapped in cellophane so thick it looks like glass. The nurse smiles at Paul, and for a moment he thinks the flowers are for Dodie, a surprise his father has planned. He looks at his father, dressed in a silver suit that matches his hair exactly. His tie is patterned with tiny scales of justice, his tie clip a gold gavel, and though he seems very much his former self, Paul realizes that ordering flowers is beyond his father now, another thing that must be done for him. Paul decides to find out if his mother was right about the germs, and if she wasn't, to bring Dodie a dozen long-stem roses.

"Speaking of offices," says Paul, "I should check in with mine."

"I'm surprised you made it this long," laughs Dodie. "You want to use my phone?"

"No thanks. I'll spare you and Dad the shoptalk," Paul says, patting his father on the back and stepping outside.

■ ■ ■ ■

There are no flowers at the nurses' station, evidence that Paul's mother was wrong. An unshaven intern is barking orders at an older nurse, and though Paul makes his living by defending doctors, he doesn't like most of them, especially the young ones who've gone into medicine for the money, planning to retire early and sell real estate. Often Paul's clients are guilty — a botched liposuction that left dents in a thigh, imprudent anesthesia that left the patient in a coma — and what Paul argues is the amount of damages: how big was the mistake, how old was the victim. He's read enough charts and deciphered enough prescriptions to learn that nurses know what's best for a patient, so he searches the swarm of white uniforms for a splash of yellow, the color of the cardigan worn by the nurse who passed Dodie's door, until he sees her making notes at the counter.

"Excuse me," says Paul, touching her yellow shoulder. The nurse seems irritated as she turns around, but she smiles when she sees Paul. "I was wondering if Dodie Olsen in 305 is allowed to get flowers."

The nurse looks confused.

"There's no worry about germs or anything?" he asks.

"Not at all," she says, smiling again, leaning against the counter as though it's a bar.

"Or maybe a plant?" suggests Paul, as if she's a salesgirl helping him choose a gift for Grace. "Something Miss Olsen could take home with her."

"I think she'd prefer flowers," the nurse says, in a way that makes Paul think Dodie might not make it out of the hospital.

She directs him through the maze of wings and wards to a florist in the lobby. Paul walks slowly, remembering his father's long stay in the hospital. His mother was sober for most of it, sleeping in the next bed, rising at dawn to rush home for a change of clothes and returning before his father awoke. One morning she arrived late and loaded, and though Paul checked her purse and searched her pockets for a hidden bottle, he didn't find one. It wasn't until he was out of the room, walking his father along the corridor, that his youngest brother, Freddy, discovered the liquor, smuggled in a stack of clean pajamas his mother had brought from home. Paul and his father had walked as far as the visitors' lounge, but Paul could hear Freddy's screams, his mother's sobs, the sound of shattering glass. When they returned to the room, it reeked of bourbon, and an orderly was sweeping up shards of glass from a broken bottle and from a vase that had held the flowers Dodie had sent the day before.

Paul stops at a pay phone, punching in numbers and waiting for it to ring. He wishes he could tell the receptionist to read him only the important messages, but after three years she still can't tell what's important and what's not.

"Where are you?" she asks.

"Georgetown Hospital. I told you I'd be out today."

"Are you okay?" Her Baltimore accent mutilates the word "okay," stretching the "o," swallowing the "ay." It is the one aspect of Baltimore Paul still doesn't like.

"Fine," says Paul. "Visiting a friend. Any calls?"

Paul listens to her read the pink slips. He hangs up the phone when she's finished, immediately picking it up again and dialing his home number. Grace answers on the first ring.

"How's it going?" she asks.

"Okay. Weird."

"Weird is par for the course with your father," says Grace. "Did he even ask about his newest grandchildren?"

"He can't remember that he has new grandchildren."

"Then why can't he forget how we met," asks Grace, "and accept me as your wife? I've managed to melt your mother."

"Give him time," Paul tells her. "He's old."

"The twins will be too by the time your father meets them," she says, and a baby cries in the background. "Sounds like someone heard me mention their phantom grandfather."

"Grace..."

"I don't understand why you're so nice to your father. He's not very nice to you."

"That's not fair," says Paul. "You didn't know him before the stroke."

"You did?" she asks, both babies now crying. "Gotta go. I'm sorry, Paul, I just love you so much."

"I love you too," he tells her, pressing the receiver down and remembering how his father used to be, his eyes darker than Paul's, lively, and sometimes mean. His father always wore dark glasses indoors, and though Paul's now grateful to the impenetrable lens for hiding his father's dazed look, Paul can recall a sunny kitchen in an apartment, before the move to their first house, before his siblings were born, when the sunglasses seemed like a barrier, his father's eyes lost behind them like marbles in muddy water.

He doesn't know who to call next. There were two messages that mattered, one from a doctor, another from an insurance company, but this is a rare day off, and Paul doesn't feel like discussing death and damages, so he slips those phone numbers into his pocket and pulls out a quarter to call his mother. The coin clinks inside the pay phone and the dial tone clicks on, but Paul does not dial: his mother's been sober for several months, and though she claims that it's nothing more than a diet, a caloric concern, he doesn't want anything to trigger her, doesn't want his mother to know that his father is alone with Dodie. The dial tone becomes a loud beep and Paul hangs up.

■ ■ ■ ■

The florist has a variety of beautifully colored roses to choose from, but Paul selects an assortment of tulips and lilies arranged in a rustic jug, friendly yet not romantic. Paul doesn't know what to write on the small gift card, and though he wants to sign his father's name, to tell Dodie the flowers were his father's idea, instead he scribbles something about great affection and getting well, signing it, "The Donovans." The florist warns him to walk slowly so the water won't spill, and when Paul finally approaches Dodie's door, he hears his father.

"I brought you a get-well gift," his father is saying.

"You didn't have to do that, Mr. D."

Paul stops. The door to Dodie's room is open and Paul can see his father, though Paul can tell from the blank stare that his father can't see him. He watches his father fumble with the pocket of his topcoat, pulling something out and handing it to Dodie, whose face is out of Paul's view.

"I thought you'd enjoy this," his father says, "though I remember having difficulty reading while I was hospitalized."

Dodie says nothing.

"I inscribed the title page," his father continues, "if you can still read my handwriting."

"Of course I can," she says, reading it so softly that Paul can't hear what words his father wrote.

Paul thinks of the many gifts his father gave Paul's mother: an emerald ring, a satin robe, a mink stole, all of them returned. It wasn't his taste she objected to: his mother felt she didn't deserve such dazzling gifts, and though his parents argued the point, his father finished each anniversary, every birthday, all Christmases a defeated man, and Paul can tell by his father's befuddled smile how much Dodie's acceptance of this seemingly tiny token means to him.

"You are an Elizabeth Barrett Browning fan, aren't you?" his father asks Dodie. "My memory..."

"It's perfect," she says. "She's my Perry Mason."

"Somewhat more poetic," his father laughs.

"Oh yes, especially her sonnets," says Dodie, quoting, "'What I do and what I dream include thee, as the wine must taste of its own grapes. And when I sue God for myself...'"

"'He hears that name of thine,'" his father finishes, "'and sees within my eyes the tears of two.'"

Paul leans against the concrete wall, still holding the flowers. The florist has stapled a bouquet of pastel bows to the top of the plastic, and Paul worries that the arrangement will overwhelm the fading photo of the soldier on Dodie's small table or, worse, undermine his father's small gift. He tears off the card, hiding it in his pocket, and looks for someplace to put the flowers, spotting his nurse at her station.

"Aren't these Miss Olsen's flowers?" the nurse asks, surprised when he sets them on the counter.

"They're for you. For all the nurses," he says, heading back toward Dodie's room, then turning around. "They're from my father, for treating Miss Olsen so kindly."

His father is standing next to the bed when Paul comes in. His coat is on, and he looks tired. So does Dodie, dark circles under her eyes beginning to show through her makeup. Next to the framed snapshot on her night table is a leather-bound book that Paul recognizes immediately from his father's library. The title is embossed in gold, *Sonnets from the Portuguese*, and Paul remembers being confused when he first found it tucked away on a top shelf, wondering if his father spoke Portuguese until Paul opened the book and discovered it was written in a language he understood.

"Thank you for playing chauffeur," Dodie says to Paul.

"Beats practicing law any day," he tells her. "You take care of yourself, Dodie."

Paul kisses her on the cheek, and steps outside. When his father comes out a few minutes later, he is wearing his sunglasses.

■ ■ ■ ■

They sit in the car with the motor running, waiting for the cold air blasting through the vents to turn warm. His father lights a cigar.

"Our little secret," his father says.

"An occasional smoke won't hurt you, Dad."

"I've given everything else up," sighs his father. "Booze, butter..."

Paul wonders what else his father gave up. He wants to say something about Dodie, knowing that anything more than her medical condition might be too painful for his mother to hear.

"It meant a lot to Dodie, your going to see her."

"I wish I'd gone before," says his father. "She's had a hard life. Now this."

The car is warm now, but smoky, so Paul cracks his window, feeling the sting of winter air. He waits, sensing his father has more to say.

"Scholarship student at Brooklyn College," his father tells him. "Dropped out when she got engaged. Her young man was killed in Korea. That's when she moved to Washington. That's when I met her."

His father stops there, reaching over and laying his hand on top of Paul's. A weekly manicure keeps his father's nails gleaming, but his fingers are coarse and dry, the three diamonds on his wedding ring looking out of place on his father's workmanlike hands. The gold band feels cold against Paul's skin, and Paul wishes he were someone who could know things about a person merely by touching their jewelry.

Paul sees the hospital in his rearview mirror as he backs out, uncomfortable driving in reverse. His father's head is turned, as if he's trying to locate Dodie's room, though he can barely see and the windows are tinted so that patients can see out of them but no one can see in, like the dark glasses his father is wearing despite the setting sun. The windows used to be clear, and Paul remembers coming here when Freddy was born, almost three decades ago. He stood in the parking lot, too young to be a visitor, his left hand holding his father's and his right waving to his mother. She was four stories up, which seemed high then, holding his newborn brother to the glass so Paul could see him. Afterwards, he and his father celebrated at a nearby bar that no longer exists, where Paul learned how to eat an oyster, smoke a cigar, and sprinkle salt in flat beer to make it fizz, and though Paul was frightened that someone might steal Freddy, his father assured him the nurses would protect the baby, protect Paul's mother. Paul doesn't know what assurance he can offer his father or what protection he can provide, merely the comfort of a son's presence, and perhaps an unspoken prayer that Dodie will die peacefully, the men she might have married waiting next to her on the night table, where a young soldier is guarding the sonnets Paul's father brought.

TATTOO

Belle Bernstein's tattoo is hidden low enough on her hip that her bikini underwear covers it, but on the third night of her visit, she shows it to Freddy.

"I've only had it for two weeks," she tells him, pulling down one side of her panties to reveal her tattoo, round like a button, purple like a bruise. It resembles the face of a smiling baby, but the tiny red stars above clearly make it the moon. "I'd wanted one for a long time."

"How long?" he asks.

"Six months," she says. "At least."

Six months is a long time to Belle Bernstein, who in the thirteen years since she and Freddy graduated high school has attended five colleges, lived in seven cities in three countries, slept with countless men, and fallen in love with many of them, the longest of these relationships lasting less than six months. Freddy has lived in one city, New York, where he is an actor like he always said he'd be, and he's loved one man, though Belle is sure there've been others, many others, if not during his years with Mark, then before and after.

"What finally persuaded you?" asks Freddy.

Dick Scanlan

"A bargain," Belle laughs. "Unlike you, I've never been one to purchase impulsively."

"Comparison shopping for tattoos?"

"Absolutely. I stopped every tattooed person I passed, and in New Orleans there are many."

"I can imagine," says Freddy. "Men with 'Mom' on their biceps."

"No, Freddy. Far more fanciful drawings, like neon crawfish, elaborate dragons. And not just men. A lesbian I work with has a collage of colorful flowers and feminist symbols along her inner thighs."

"Well, yours is fabulous," Freddy tells her. He doesn't touch her tattoo like most people do, but he is smiling, and Belle notices what a handsome man he's grown into, the tiny lines around his eyes making him no longer pretty, though his hair is still thick and blond.

"I was afraid to show it to you," she confesses.

"Bebe," he laughs, and though it is a name she left behind long ago, it sounds good to hear him say it.

■ ■ ■ ■

She does not know who put her initials together and came up with Bebe, though growing up, that's what she was called. It certainly wasn't her mother, who, despite her politically correct commitment to zero population growth, had begged her husband for a third chance after giving birth to two boys. Though it was against their beliefs (and way out of their budget), he agreed, and finally she had her daughter, naming her Belle, the French word for beauty.

But Belle was never beautiful, even as a baby. She was a chubby little girl, and people used to marvel at the resemblance between her and her mother, making Belle cringe, for her mother was fat. Eventually even her mother called her Bebe, as if she'd named her Belle as a prophecy, abandoning the name as Belle grew into a plain and pudgy child with a round, low belly, making her look a few months pregnant long before she'd gone through puberty.

The decision to lose Bebe and become Belle happened suddenly, in bed with the only man who had ever loved her. She was at college number one, an expensive university in Chicago Belle was smart enough to get into but not smart enough to get money out of. She knew she'd be able to afford only one year no matter how many tables she waited on, but she tried, and it was at the restaurant that she met Wally. He was a construction worker ("The kind that makes a lot of money," she told Freddy long-distance. "He drives a 280Z."), ten years older than she and determined to marry her from their first date. Lying in his bed after making love, Belle felt far away from her dorm, her family, Freddy. Wally played with her hair, which was short, coarse, and dark, not the kind of hair people liked to play with. One night he asked her what Bebe was short for, and when she told him, he repeated it, whispering, "Belle," into her ear as if it was a secret. She closed her eyes, and her hair in his fingers felt fine and blonde and beautiful.

■ ■ ■ ■

"Did you and Mark used to come here?" asks Belle.

They are at an Afghani restaurant near Freddy's apartment. It is small, dark, and dirty, and Belle is eating chicken with her fingers.

Freddy shakes his head. "This is my single-man restaurant. Mark cooked."

"And when he was sick?"

"I kept him cooking as long as I could," laughs Freddy, "if you know what I mean."

They've always talked openly about sex: gay, straight, romantic, or raunchy. Belle spent two years talking about it as a social worker who dealt with sex in the school system, returning to the high school she and Freddy attended to teach her former teachers how to handle teenage sexuality. She considers her first sexual experience to have been a vicarious one through Freddy, who lost his heterosexual virginity in her room, on her bed, with her best friend. Moments later Belle had sat on the edge of the bed and discussed every detail, a single candle lighting the darkened room. Freddy did most of the talking, but Belle was more interested in their bodies, which were tangled together, Freddy's torso tanned and skinny, her friend's breasts firm and flawless, like the paintings of perfect women Belle had seen in museums, or the centerfolds in the porno magazines her parents hid under their bed.

Freddy is angrily gesturing to the waiter for water. He has come directly from a temp job, looking more like a lawyer than a typist in his charcoal gray suit. There are other elegantly dressed men here, most of them with women, sitting at tiny tables that line the narrow room, underneath dated maps of Afghanistan, faded fabrics, batiked and woven and draped along the length of the walls. A huge, horrible portrait of Ronald Reagan is hanging over Freddy's head. Freddy told her that he comes here because the food is good, but he can't stand the service. Tonight their meal was served before the silverware, and they still haven't gotten their drinks though they're halfway through their spicy dinners.

"I like this place," says Belle. "It's what I'm used to. Strictly Third World."

"New Orleans is hardly Third World."

"You haven't seen my apartment."

"You're working in a hospital. Don't they have rich doctors down there?"

"I was seeing one last spring," she tells him. "A surgeon, no less. I thought he was Mr. Right, Freddy. We were such great friends."

"Shared interests?" asks Freddy.

"Of course," Belle says. "He had those good liberal values."

"And a good income to match."

"The things we liked didn't cost money. We would stay up all night talking, making love. Sometimes he'd hold me and I would weep in his arms."

"About?"

"I'm not sure, because I never cry. Never. Except with him." Belle takes a sip of water, which the waiter has finally served. "I'm making more of it than it probably was. We were only involved for five months."

"Five months is significant," says Freddy.

"You had five years."

Freddy shrugs. "It felt like a few minutes."

Belle places her hand over his, but what she feels is failure. She works in an AIDS ward, and though the patients are her primary concern, much of her time is spent comforting their grieving lovers. Yet here, with her oldest friend, she can find no words to soothe his sadness or fend off his fear. She takes her hand away, knowing that no gesture is better than an empty one.

"Did your mother meet the surgeon?" Freddy asks.

"Oh yes. And she liked him, but they don't pressure me that way. My mother says she just wants me to be happy."

"That's nice."

"But not normal. She should want me to be married. Maybe she knows something I don't, like I'm not marriage material."

"You haven't met the right man yet," says Freddy, offering her his plate. "Lamb?"

Belle picks up her fork, which she hasn't used during dinner, spears the morsel of meat, and brings it to her mouth.

"Yours is better," she says, chewing. "My chicken's good but your lamb is better."

"So what happened to Dr. Right?"

"He went to Japan for a month to study a new surgical technique, and he came back with a new girlfriend. I knew something was up when I stopped getting the daily phone calls from Tokyo, but he didn't tell me until he'd been back for a week. He avoided me at the hospital, dodged my calls. Then one night he showed up at my house with some perfume, which he said was from Japan but was obviously a last-minute purchase at the duty-free shop."

"And what did he say?"

"You know. Blah, blah, blah, couldn't help himself, blah, blah, blah, still be best friends, blah, blah, blah, nothing's changed between us. We went that night to a jazz club, listened to music, held hands. It was great, until we got back to my place at four a.m. and he started to undress, ready to spend the night and not have sex."

"Did you have a breakdown?"

"More like a freak-out. I started pulling his clothes from my closet, screaming, 'Out of my house,' over and over again. He kept telling me that nothing had changed, and the more he said it, the madder I got."

"Because it's bullshit," says Freddy.

"Because it's true. It was easy for him not to sleep with me: he'd never wanted me as a woman. He wants what all men want: a beautiful wife to take care of their beautiful house and beautiful children."

The waiter gives Freddy the check, though Freddy hasn't asked for it and Belle's buying dinner. She tries to take it from him, but Freddy holds onto her hand.

"You're too hard on yourself, Belle Bernstein," he says. "Sounds like you're better off without this guy."

"After he left I drove two hours to the boonies of Louisiana and parked at a lake where we used to go on weekends. It was the perfect place to sob, with the sky that bruised predawn purple, but I couldn't shed a tear. I couldn't weep without him."

"I know that feeling," Freddy tells her. She turns around to get her purse, and is surprised to see a line, men with men, men with women, men with wine or beer since this place serves no liquor. The front couple seems angry at the wait, and at the waiters, as if they've been here before. Belle counts out her money, and despite Freddy's protests about the bad service, she leaves a big tip.

■ ■ ■ ■

Belle has slept through her alarm and Freddy's departure, slept until the bright autumn sun shifted from the bedroom to the living room, where she's lying on Freddy's large sofa. The sun hurts her eyes as if she's hung over, though they drank nothing last night, and she feels even worse when she realizes that the session she's missing this morning is on abortion. Officially she's come to this public-health conference as an AIDS educator, but living in the state that tried to outlaw abortion even in rape and incest cases, she'd hoped to learn more about the legal issues surrounding it. There is little Belle doesn't already know about abortion's medical or emotional ramifications.

This is the first time she's spent alone in Freddy's apartment. It is a high-rise, all windows, which she has enjoyed looking out of, admiring Freddy's fabulous view. But this morning it occurs to her that the people she's watching might be watching her, that it's not a one-way mirror like in a department store dressing room but a sheet of glass that anyone can see through. She moves away from the windows, sitting in the kitchen drinking coffee that she brought Freddy as a gift. Even out of the sun his apartment is warm, almost like summer inside, though it is probably colder out than it ever gets in New Orleans.

She is struck by how clean his apartment is. One of the first things she learned about Freddy when they were paired as lab partners in tenth grade was that he lived in a dirty house. They'd met briefly the year before when Belle did makeup for the musical, but she was stationed in the chorus dressing room, and even as a freshman, Freddy was not in the chorus. So their friendship really began with Biology, and an experiment in which they had placed petri dishes in fifteen different locations: five in Freddy's house, five in Belle's, and five in the school building. After two weeks they viewed the cultures under a microscope, and with the help of Belle's father, who was a scientist, they analyzed the results, identifying any bacteria they found. No microscope was needed to find the bacteria from Freddy's house: it had grown green and fuzzy. Belle's father studied it for a long time, unable to say exactly what it was.

Belle is getting dressed. Through the windows she sees people bundled up in big sweaters, which, living in Louisiana, she doesn't own. She decides to borrow one from Freddy, opening his dresser drawers till she finds his sweaters, evenly stacked and neatly folded. She reaches her hand inside, running it over the different fabrics, from tightly woven to loosely knit, soft wools to bulky cottons. Underneath one of the piles her fingers feel something like shelving paper, but there are pages, and she realizes before she's pulled it out that it's a porno magazine. She opens it to a spread called "Tattooed Buddies," two bearded, muscular men whose arms are covered with tattoos and whose bodies are locked together in every position imaginable, though through it all their penises aren't fully erect. She turns to another part of the magazine, and photos fall on the floor, Polaroids of Freddy. She recognizes the man he's having sex with as Mark, though she met him only once when he was already very sick.

Freddy found Mark while Belle was in the Peace Corps, working with the poor in far-off lands. Occasionally she'd get a long letter from him, and it was in one of these twenty-page sagas that she first heard about Mark, how they met and moved in together. Soon after that she received a present from Freddy, a coffee-table book on personal style. There was no coffee table in her adobe hut to hold the book, and as she flipped through the thick pages illustrated with sample table settings and wedding invitations, she decided to let go of Freddy as she'd let go of every other friend from high school.

She did not answer his letters or respond to the messages he left with her parents. She did not speak with him until long after she'd left the Peace Corps and moved to New Orleans. Belle had come to New York for a pro-choice rally, and though she hadn't written Freddy for years, she stopped in front of an elegant building whose address she recognized as his. She entered the lobby, thinking if the doorman stopped her she'd turn and run. He didn't, and she got on the elevator, sailing up the eighteen flights as if Freddy was expecting her. She couldn't wait to see his face when he opened the door, but the face she saw was stained with purple lesions. At first she thought it was Freddy, and though she saw AIDS victims every day at work, Belle was unable to speak.

"Can I help you?" the man said, his voice sounding too healthy for his frail body, as if it were being dubbed. "What was it you wanted?"

She stood there mute, and he was about to close the door when Freddy appeared in the foyer, golden and healthy, screaming when he saw her. She was ushered in, fawned over, and fed lunch. On his coffee table was the same book he'd sent her. She didn't tell him how much she'd hated it. Instead, she described how the women in her village used to pore over each page, the luxuriousness of it comforting them in ways which Belle could never understand.

■ ■ ■ ■

They take a long walk out of Freddy's neighborhood. The night air is brisk, but they've had too much wine, which keeps them warm. Belle is wearing a leather jacket that belonged to Mark. She likes the way it fits: much too big, though Mark had a slight build. Her arm is linked tightly through Freddy's. Even so, she's sure no one would mistake them for a couple.

"That dinner was good," says Freddy.

Belle had cooked Cajun style for him tonight, using the special mix and Creole mustard she brought with her to have jambalaya waiting when he got home from work.

"You'd love New Orleans," she tells him.

"Southern charm?"

Belle shakes her head.

"It's much wilder than that. More like if it feels good, do it. Over and over again."

"That's dangerous these days."

"Which is why I was hired," says Belle. "Spreading the word about safer sex."

"Is there such a thing?" Freddy asks. "Rubbers do break."

"I learned that in the Peace Corps." Freddy looks at her. "I was sleeping with a man from the next village."

"A native?"

"A gorgeous Guatemalan. One night the rubber slipped off. Of course, I think he knew and came inside me anyway. The moment I realized, I panicked, but I had no spermicidal jelly, nothing. It's not like there are drugstores in the Guatemalan mountains."

"So what happened?"

"I had an abortion."

"There?"

"No. The Peace Corps flew me home. But before I went, I hitchhiked to his village to tell him I was pregnant. I got a ride from a lovely old man, and as we were entering town we passed José, the father of my child, in his pickup truck. I told the old man to follow him, and he did. José drove fast, but that man stayed right behind him, whizzing along the mountain roads, not asking any questions. Finally we cut him off, and when I hopped out of the car, I saw why José was in a hurry."

Freddy has his arm around her now. Two men walk past them, holding hands. Belle wonders if it's her Freddy's holding onto, or Mark's coat.

"I said it right in front of his new girlfriend," she continues. "She didn't seem to care, and he was just pissed about the car chase. I screamed it at him in Spanish. That's when I finally knew I was fluent."

She follows Freddy into an expensive-looking restaurant. Belle is uncomfortable ordering only coffee and dessert, but the hostess, a blue-eyed, blonde-haired beauty, flashes them a smile and makes it okay. She leads them to a table by the window, and immediately a waitress appears with bluer eyes, blonder hair, and a brighter smile.

"I feel like I'm in another country," says Belle, staring at the waitress as she lists desserts Belle's never heard of: *crème brulee, tirami sù, tart tatin,* which Freddy tells her is just apple pie. She orders that and Freddy gets *tirami sù,* and they eat in silence, focusing their attention on their desserts. Halfway through, they offer each other a bite. Freddy declines but Belle takes a taste of his *tirami sù*.

"I can't believe it," she says. "You did it again."

"What?"

"Made the better choice. This is delicious."

The waitress clears their plates and freshens their coffee. Freddy is looking out the window. Belle wonders if he's seeing ghosts. She leans forward, Mark's jacket draped over her shoulders.

"So what kind of sex are you having these days?" asks Belle. "I'm asking as a friend and a health-care worker."

"Not much."

"You don't take any risks, do you?"

"It's hardly worth it considering the stakes," he says. "And as you know, rubbers aren't foolproof, so penetration is a thing of the past."

"That was my policy for years after the abortion. Most men were terrible about it, calling me a tease, but I didn't want to get pregnant again."

"What about a diaphragm?"

"I can never put it in right. Do you believe that?" she asks. "It's embarrassing. I have a master's degree in public health and I can't put in a diaphragm. But last spring..."

"The surgeon?"

"He was a doctor, for God's sake. He knew how to deal with a diaphragm."

"Penetration at last!" says Freddy, his actor's voice carrying throughout their section of the restaurant. Everyone laughs, including Belle who is choking on her coffee. Freddy is not embarrassed, laughing louder and longer than anyone else except Belle, who finally sputters and hiccups to a halt. She feels drained and lightheaded, as if she's been weeping.

"I'm having an affair," she tells Freddy.

"Good for you."

"As in married man."

"Older?"

"Our age, and married less than a year. He comes to New Orleans once a month for business."

"And pleasure," says Freddy. "Do you love him?"

"It's just a fling, but I feel guilty. I remember you and I vowing to never knowingly sleep with a married man."

"I won't hold it against you, Bebe. I've broken every vow I ever made."

"I don't see how," Belle says.

"Because I don't show you how. There are some things I don't show anyone. Except Mark."

She wants to tell him that she's seen the pictures, his face flushed, his hair sweaty, his mouth filled with Mark. But Freddy is standing up, ready to leave.

"Let's take a taxi," he tells her as they step into the cold night. "I'm suddenly very tired."

■ ■ ■ ■

Freddy sighs, grunts, and groans on the bed, his body melting from Belle's massage.

"This is wonderful," he says, his voice muffled, his face buried in a pillow.

"I've been told I'm good." She coats her hands with more lotion and returns to his shoulders, digging her thumbs into his neck. "This was the extent of my sex life with Louis."

"The diplomat you dated?"

"Yeah. He never wanted to have intercourse."

"That's a problem," Freddy says.

"I think he was gay. He adored you."

"I liked him, I think. It was so long ago now."

"Did you sleep with him?" asks Belle.

"Of course not."

"But he made a pass at you, didn't he?" Her hands are clenched in fists, pressing against his lower back with full force, but it doesn't seem to hurt him.

"No," says Freddy, turning his head to look at her. "Bebe, I barely knew him."

She works her way up his spine as if her fingers are climbing a ladder.

"I've been thinking a lot about old boyfriends lately. I even called Wally on my thirtieth birthday."

"Which one was Wally?"

"I can't believe you don't remember," says Belle, her hands recoiling from his skin.

"I'm sorry. The construction worker?"

"The one man who wanted to marry me. And if I'd known then what I know now about love..."

"You still wouldn't have married him," Freddy tells her. "He wasn't smart enough."

"Does that matter?" she asks. "We hadn't spoken in years when I called. A woman answered the phone, his wife, and as soon as I said my name she knew who I was. Wally took the call in the bedroom, the door closed, and he wished me happy thirtieth before I even told him it was my birthday. He still dreams about me, Freddy. He told me he saved every picture. That's the kind of impact I want to have on a man."

Without realizing it, Belle is touching Freddy again, though barely, her fingertips grazing his back, straying into his hair. She sits there long after he's fallen asleep, lonely not for Wally but for Wally's feelings for her. She looks at Freddy's narrow shoulders, his long torso, and wonders what it is he misses most about Mark.

■ ■ ■ ■

Belle is shopping, surprised that she's able to find clothes in New York that don't exceed her $50 per outfit budget. She buys things she won't wear to work: three black-and-white dresses (more dresses than she currently owns) that are too tailored and not colorful enough for the drab clinic; perfect for a wedding, a dinner party, a date. The skirts she found on special are almost insultingly bright, the kind of cheerful that makes sick people feel worse.

They are full-cut and flowing, and Belle imagines how they will billow about her as she twirls.

She did not used to dance. During the disco days, she'd sit at a table sipping a soft drink and watching Freddy on the dance floor, his hair big and blown dry, his choreographed precision intimidating her. He told her it's been years since he went to a club, but Belle spends most Saturdays Cajun dancing.

"Is that what they taught us in high school gym?" asked Freddy.

"That was square dancing," she told him. "This is sexier."

"Like the two-step?"

She tried to demonstrate in his living room, but it felt lifeless and flat, for it is a dance in which the man supplies the power. She showed him photos from the last festival she attended, a weekend of beer, blackened fish, and dancing all day, all night. Her skirt was hitched up on one side, and she had a different partner in every picture, but she looked happy with all of them. Freddy only asked the names of the men she was kissing, which she explained was part of the dance. There were many pictures of her "sacrificing a watermelon," hurling it onto the ground, then falling on her knees and eating the huge pieces it had broken into. Watermelon juice dripped down her neck, staining her t-shirt, but in the pictures it looked like sweat.

She heads back toward the hotel for the closing ceremonies of the conference. She skipped this morning's talk on "Public Health in the Year 2000": Belle has enough private fears about where she'll be in ten years, whether she'll still be alone, whether Freddy will still be alive. Normally she'd feel guilty about missing a meeting, but she's enjoying her spree, admiring her glossy shopping bags topped with peaks of pastel tissue paper, like colored whipped cream.

There are no old people on the street, and New Orleans is full of them. The younger generation there is moving away, for it is a dying city, though it continues to be vital and proud, much like the patients Belle works with. She cannot imagine being old in

New York, or sick. Or single. Down south, Belle is considered cute and thin. She's lost a lot of weight since high school (though Freddy's always saying, "You look exactly the same," as if it's a compliment), but she still has her belly, and here, where women don't get married at eighteen and have a child at twenty, she'd feel fat. She remembers feeling beautiful in Guatemala, her features delicate, her skin fair next to the dark, wide faces of the native women.

Belle sees faces like that lined up outside the hotel, a large crowd of maids and bellboys. At first she thinks it's a strike, since this hotel is famous for mistreating its employees, but then she recognizes colleagues from the conference. As she gets closer, she sees a police barricade and shattered glass, and she hears the Hispanic women wailing with pain, the kind of cries Belle's heard after the birth of a stillborn baby or the death of an AIDS victim.

"Se matò," one of the maids is chanting, "se matò, ella se matò..."

Belle knows before she looks that there will be a body, a maid who minutes before was making a bed or scrubbing a toilet. She wonders why the maid jumped, remembering how bravely the women in Guatemala bore their poverty, working sixteen-hour days to barely feed their children. She thinks of her patients in the AIDS ward. Clients, they're called, mostly young men who Belle helps hang on for one more week, one more day, until their pain becomes too great and Belle begs them to let go. Maybe that's what the maid did, her spirit soaring overhead as her body lies on the ground, covered by a sheet. Belle looks up at the high-rise hotel, trying to find the window from which the maid jumped. She spots it immediately, the window with no glass left making all the others look filthy.

■ ■ ■ ■

They go to a small gallery filled with Latin American art. There are no prices on the paintings, but Belle overhears a well-dressed young man quietly tell some Texans that the most recent work by this artist went for fifteen thousand. The Texans think that's a bargain, but Belle knows these dark and decorative paintings would be worthless in Guatemala, where $15,000 could feed her entire village for months.

Freddy doesn't feel well, his stomach still recovering from her Cajun cooking. She finds him sitting on a green leather sofa that resembles a car seat, surrounded by portraits of mustached women with melancholy eyes.

"I like this stuff," he says.

"I'm surprised."

"You underestimate me," he tells her. "Does it make you want to go back?"

"To Guatemala?" He nods. "I did, for a week last year. It was incredible," she says, sitting down. "Babies I'd helped enter this world are now little people. One of them is named after me. Oh Freddy, she's a beauty."

"They must have adored you there."

"They did. It was like a holiday when I returned."

"After Mark died I took a trip to France. We'd been there together," he tells her. "It's nice going back to places."

"Not always," says Belle. "I went to Germany with my grandmother. Her hometown had invited back all the Jews that had once lived there."

"The few that survived," he says. "I never knew your grandmother had been in a death camp."

"She wasn't. She was able to leave the country in 1938 on a technicality. My grandfather had some Czechoslovakian blood," Belle explains. "But across the aisle from us on the flight over was a friend of hers who'd been sent to Dachau, a woman she hadn't seen in fifty years. I could see the tattoo. It looked like a phone number written on her forearm. I think my grandmother felt guilty."

"Because she hadn't suffered as much as her friend?"

"No, because she had. Just in living a normal life, my grandmother felt she'd known all the sadness a human heart can know.

Yet she had nothing to show for it, no number on her arm to point to and blame."

Belle starts to stand, but Freddy tugs on her sleeve, still feeling sick.

"You've always had a nervous stomach," she tells him. "Even in high school."

"Especially in high school," he laughs, but she knows he is frightened. They've both seen firsthand how something as ordinary as an upset stomach can mean the beginning of death. She sits next to him, holding his hand. They try to talk about the large, messy painting that's facing them, but they're too close to it to get any perspective. Finally Freddy rises, and Belle follows him outside.

It is drizzling, Freddy's least favorite weather, so they don't walk far though Belle likes this part of town. The streets are narrower, the buildings lower, too low for anyone to leap out of. They look for a restaurant, but it is that strange time of day when lunch is over and dinner not yet begun. Instead, they go to a bar, where Freddy can find a bathroom. Belle sits on a bar stool, bums a cigarette from the bartender, and orders herself a beer.

She should not be smoking. She should not be drinking. Belle's done many things she should not have since the at-home pregnancy test showed a red stain as impossible to ignore as an AIDS victim's first lesion and, in the case of her unborn baby, as inevitable a death sentence. She shouldn't have called the married man at home to tell him, or been surprised when he said he was really there for her but could he call her tomorrow from the office.

The tattoo, however, she does not regret. The day after she discovered she was pregnant, she went to a tattoo convention, though she wasn't sure she'd actually get one. Belle looked at hundreds of tattoos done by dozens of artists, but it wasn't until she saw Sister Bear's work that she made up her mind. It was all deep purples, dark reds, and Belle wanted it right on the belly. Sister Bear suggested the hip, where Belle would be less likely to gain weight and distort the tattoo, misshaping the moon's face. It took longer and hurt more than Belle had thought it would, and a crowd of men gathered to watch.

An older woman tries to sit next to her.

"I'm waiting for someone," Belle says, holding out her hand to save the seat for Freddy. She thinks about telling him when he returns. He would listen to her failed attempts at this week's conference to get her hands on the French pill that terminates pregnancy privately, with no pain. He'd understand, she imagines, probably offering to go with her next week when she meets her married man in a state she doesn't live in so she can get an abortion from a doctor she doesn't know.

She hears the bathroom door open and turns to see Freddy. He looks handsome. He looks healthy, but he is not who she is waiting for. She's waiting for one of the men who saw the moon appear on her hip, any one of the men. Freddy climbs up on the stool next to her, feeling better he says, but Belle is barely listening, holding onto her memory of those men as Freddy might take a final hurried glance at the photos of him and Mark while someone's knocking on his door. She sees herself lying there long after the moon is full and finished, her hip exposed, a towel draped over the rest of her body. The men are touching her tattoo, and in that moment she is dizzy, not from the beers they keep bringing her, but lightheaded, lighthearted, with hope.

DOES FREDDY DANCE

"Do you remember this morning when I said I was thinking about you?" Neil asks.

Freddy nods. He had called Neil this morning to confirm their date. He heard music in the background. There's always music in the background when he calls Neil's apartment, even on the answering machine. He remembers Neil telling him that there's a radio in the shower.

"General thoughts?" Freddy asks.

"Actually I was lying in bed..."

Neil pauses. Under the table he slides his hand along Freddy's thigh.

"Lying in bed, and I thought, 'Does Freddy dance?'"

"What?"

"Do you dance?" Neil asks.

Freddy looks at Neil's face. It is a handsome face, though Freddy didn't realize how handsome until tonight, now that the weather's changed, now that fall's started. Maybe because Neil's coloring is the coloring of autumn: ruddy complexion, golden eyes, chestnut hair.

"I've danced in many shows," says Freddy, an auditionee answering the choreographer's question. "Jazz, ballet, tap..."

Dick Scanlan

"No," Neil says. "Partner dancing."

"Like the hustle?" Freddy asks. "Disco dancing? I used to fifteen years ago when there was still such a thing as discos."

The waiter refills Freddy's red wine before Freddy can cover his glass with his hand. He can already feel a flush burning in his cheeks, his mouth getting dry, his speech starting to slur. He pushes his wineglass away and takes a sip of water. He needs to speak clearly tonight.

"Freddy, I mean waltzing. Slow dancing."

"Oh. Yes. It's the one kind of dancing I'm naturally gifted at. Women at weddings line up to have me spin them around the floor."

"So you lead?" Neil continues.

"Sure. I took cotillion classes when I was a kid."

The soup arrives. Freddy watches Neil eat it, bringing the spoon to his mouth, curling his lips in preparation for the hot soup, like he did the first time he kissed Freddy. It was on the beach, late afternoon on the last day of Labor Day weekend, the last day of the season. They had spent a month of weekends stopping by each other's towel, rubbing suntan lotion on each other's back, staying for longer and longer visits until that weekend, when they laid their towels side by side.

"I can lead too," Neil says. "I won first place in a waltzing contest in college. I think I also placed in the jitterbug competition."

"Most men can't," says Freddy.

"Jitterbug?"

"No. Lead."

"I know."

Freddy finishes his soup and wipes his mouth with the thick, cream-colored napkin. He remembers Neil's finger on his mouth, brushing off a speck of sand. Or that's what Neil had said he was doing. He'd brought his face close to Freddy's to make sure the sand was gone, and Freddy saw his white teeth for only a moment before Neil pressed his lips against Freddy's. Freddy had forgotten how to kiss, so he mirrored Neil's tongue with his own.

"I like this restaurant," Freddy tells Neil. "It's smart."

"It suits you."

"You think? It's more East Village than I am. You know, black and blond and bright red lipstick."

"Have you been here before?"

Freddy shakes his head no, using his body to lie. He plans to speak the truth later tonight, but until then he'll enjoy the formality of a first date, how safe he feels when someone knows nothing about him. The man he had dinner with here before would know he was lying. He knew Freddy's body language: he knew Freddy's body.

Neil offers him a taste of his asparagus, cutting off the tips of three perfect pieces. They taste sweet and healthy to Freddy, who is always surprised when he likes food that is good for him.

"I've tried to follow," Neil says. They are back to ballroom dancing. "It's like trying to say your name backwards. I can't figure it out."

"You have to feel it out."

"What do you mean?" asks Neil.

"I was in a show once where I played a woman. And at the end I was crowned a beauty queen, so I had to waltz with the emcee. Like Bert Parks. Only we'd never rehearsed it. There's always something in a show that you skip in rehearsals."

"So what happened?"

"When we got to that moment on opening night, I let my body take over. I let this man sweep me around the stage. I wasn't conscious of the steps, or what I was doing. Just his arms. Just the music."

They split a parfait. It is pale pink and frozen solid, so Freddy holds the frosted glass as Neil chips away at the ice cream with a long spoon.

"It's always different seeing someone you know from the beach here in the City," says Neil, now holding the parfait glass so Freddy can have some.

"I have more clothes on, for one thing," says Freddy.

"That can be remedied."

Freddy feels himself growing hard, though flirting frightens him. It's too close to having sex, as close as Freddy's gotten in a long time, except for the kiss on the beach. He remembers Neil's mouth covering his, warm, the rest of his body cool in the setting sun.

Neil continues, embarrassed. "I guess what I'm saying is that I've liked you for a while now, Freddy. All that time on the beach, our phone conversations the past two weeks. But tonight, seeing you, I like you even more."

Freddy says nothing. The ice cream is cold and it makes his head hurt, but his throat is so tight he can't swallow.

"I have some tango records at home. And waltzes. Polkas," Neil says. "Maybe we could dance sometime."

"Maybe," Freddy mumbles. "But no polkas, please."

They walk back to Neil's apartment. The temperature has dropped, and Freddy has his hands in his pockets for warmth. Neil is talking about his neighborhood, his advertising agency, his best friend in Los Angeles. Freddy is barely listening, afraid to know things like the name of Neil's secretary or the number of Neil's siblings, afraid that after tonight he'll have only the details of Neil's life but no Neil, though Neil seems unstoppable as he mentions another restaurant they must try, a movie they must see, a friend Freddy must meet.

Neil kisses him in the elevator. He doesn't stop when they arrive on his floor, leaning on the door open button and pressing Freddy against the mirrored wall. His kisses taste of coffee and red wine, though Freddy can still recall the salty sea taste of their first kiss.

Freddy breaks free and stands in the hall, not knowing which apartment is Neil's, waiting for Neil to lead him there.

There is music playing when Neil opens his front door. Soft music. Neil switches on a dim light and Freddy looks for speakers, but can't find any. He doesn't know where the music is coming from. It is a piano piece, very modern. Freddy's never heard it before.

Neil pulls him onto the couch, gently kissing Freddy's forehead, then brushing his lips along Freddy's nose. Freddy stops him when he gets to his mouth, holding his fingers up to Neil's lips.

"There's something you should know."

"What?" asks Neil, taking Freddy's finger into his mouth as he says the word. He is smiling, as if he expects Freddy to say something funny, something sexy.

Freddy's never done this before, and despite his two weeks of worrying about how this evening would go, he does not have his lines memorized, or even written. He could just blurt it out, but instead, he decides to introduce a third party, someone Freddy can hide behind, someone Neil can blame.

"I had a boyfriend for several years," Freddy says slowly. "He died of AIDS."

Neil leans back, hands folded in his lap. Freddy sits on the edge of the sofa, ready to make a run for it.

"When?"

"A year ago May."

"Jesus," Neil says, though Freddy can't tell who he's praying for. "I'm sorry."

Freddy stares at the brightly painted Chinese bowl on the coffee table in front of him. It is filled with fortunes from inside hundreds of cookies. Some of them are bunched together, held by paper clips. Maybe by theme, he thinks. He wonders if they're all good fortunes.

"What you must have gone through," Neil says, still not touching Freddy.

Freddy searches for something to say. He keeps meaning to come up with some sort of statement, some sort of press release about what he's gone through, but it doesn't seem to come out in words.

He shrugs. "I don't know what else to say."

"Nothing," says Neil. "Unless you want to. I think that's all I need to know."

Freddy is rocking back and forth, hugging himself as if he's straitjacketed. He rocks forward onto his feet, ready to leave.

"For now," Neil whispers, standing behind him, sliding his arms around Freddy's waist.

Freddy is frozen, afraid to move, though his body starts moving anyway, following Neil, swaying from side to side. He keeps his eyes closed as Neil turns him slowly around so they are facing each other, inches apart. Freddy's heart is pounding, his mouth dry, as if this will be his first kiss, erasing the past that Freddy feared would prevent them from having a future. Neil moves closer, and Freddy almost laughs, for what he is thinking in anticipation of Neil's kiss is of Neil's three sisters and his secretary, Marianne, all the information Freddy thought he'd screened out, all the hope he'd tried to hold at bay. But the kiss doesn't come. Instead, Neil presses his cheek against Freddy's, holding Freddy tight as their feet begin to move to the music. Neil is leading, as he said he could, but his steps are tentative, and Freddy wonders how long this dance will last.

LIFE LINE

Dick Scanlan

Bunny encourages me to eat beef, though she's been a vegetarian longer than we've been friends. She uses red meat as bait, describing juicy hamburgers and rare steaks with a mouth-watering accuracy that defies her two decades' abstinence. Today it is roast beef on rye.

"Taste those paper-thin slices of pink meat," she whispers into the phone like an obscene caller, "and picture us in the Park, sipping iced coffee while you eat your sandwich."

"What are you eating?" I ask.

"Nothing," says Bunny, "because I feel fat. Gravity starts taking its toll when you turn thirty."

"Age is hell," I tell her, and she laughs because that was one of my favorite expressions the summer we met doing *West Side Story,* when I was sixteen and fond of saying, "I'm not as young as I used to be." The cast celebrated Bunny's seventeenth birthday with a surprise party during rehearsal, and amidst the cake, the cards, and the chorus of "Happy Birthday," I slipped her a shopping bag filled with skin-care products and a note saying, "The party's over, Bunny. Fight wrinkles now." We've been a part of each other's birthday ever since, the worst being Bunny's thirtieth because she was between boyfriends, single and scared of remaining so. I turned thirty a year later, also single, having lost my lover to AIDS, but I no longer have misgivings about growing older: I know my options.

"Yum," she continues, "the tomato is perfectly ripe, the lettuce crisp and cool..."

This is our own version of the Love Line, a phone sex service that supports us both by buying Bunny's sixty-second scripts in which a man makes prerecorded love to the caller, and hiring me to prerecord it. Bunny keeps coming up with new lovemaking locales, having long ago exhausted all locker-room variations. Once she had me on top of a Xerox machine, making enlarged copies of my genitalia while servicing my male secretary, but the basic formula never varies: I am always well built and willing, the other man the biggest and best, and mutual orgasm is achieved in the fifty-seventh second. We call our platonic variation the Life Line, and though it has the same breathless urgency, the source of the excitement is anything but sexual. "Hi, I'm Bunny and I'm looking for a friend," she'll say into my machine. "I'm slipping a Hitchcock tape into the VCR and pressing Play. Yeah, baby, I can smell the microwave popcorn popping as the credits roll on this classic black-and-white." The Life Line focuses on late-night activities, old movies, and forbidden food, but Bunny has a new boyfriend and I have a new show, so lately we've discovered daytime pleasures to tempt each other with: matinees, manicures, this morning a picnic.

"I can't," I tell her. "There's a reading of a new musical I should go to, and an audition for *Our Town* somewhere in the Midwest."

"Stop looking for work," says Bunny. "You've got a long run ahead."

"I hope."

"I know," she stresses. "I'm the one with things to do, like pack up this apartment, but I'd rather have lunch with you and leave that for the last minute."

Packing has been her top priority for the past week, but she still hasn't started. There are months of unpaid bills and years of letters to sort through, love letters from ex-boyfriends and long letters from me on the road, stuck underneath unfinished cups of cold coffee, bursting out of dresser drawers. Bunny and I were roommates before I met my lover, and often she'd sleep with me, unable to get through the clutter of her room to her bed. Sometimes in the middle of the night I would mount her, rubbing my flannel nightshirt against hers until she hit me hard enough to wake me up, accusing me of being a closet heterosexual. Living alone in a small studio has made Bunny less messy, but her apartment's not nearly ready for the summer tenant to take over.

She has sublet it to a young actor with piercing blue eyes, a big date book that he's constantly checking, and the kind of confidence that comes from thinking he'll live forever yet never hit thirty. I was there the day he came to look at her place, and though I have one of the bigger roles in the biggest hit off-Broadway this season, he had no use for me. He measured the room, the bathroom, the closets, scribbling the dimensions in his oversized organizer and asking, "Is there a possibility of this becoming a long term sublet situation?" Bunny didn't respond, busy counting the twenty one-hundred-dollar bills with which he'd paid a full summer's rent, making their arrangement seem somehow illicit.

Bunny continues her pitch, a salesman on a roll. "Two more days and we'll have to rely solely on the Life Line," she says, "with no chance to live out our fantasies except when I come to New York for the day, like a suburban housewife on a spree."

"I've already applied for credit cards at Philly's leading department stores," I say. "The moment they come I intend to train down and take you out for a leisurely lunch and a waxing at Wanamaker's."

"I'm afraid you'll be disappointed in Wanamaker's," Bunny tells me. "Peter says it's a dying department store."

Peter is the new boyfriend, a lawyer in Philadelphia she found at a party here in New York. He's been traveling the eighty miles almost daily for the past seven months, but Bunny has decided to spend the summer with him in Philly, sunbathing in his backyard, writing fiction in a sun-filled spare bedroom. Peter had his secretary send me a packet of credit card applications to Philadelphia stores, with a typed note extending me an all-summer, open invitation to his house. He's tried to prepare me for my visit, worried that I'll be bored in what he admits is a second-rate city. I'm worried that Bunny won't be.

I have one more appointment for the Life Line to handle, hoping Bunny will tell me to postpone it.

"I'm also supposed to see my doctor."

Bunny says nothing. She never talks about my health, despite the obvious implications of my boyfriend's death, but in her version of the future I am there, with a new man and plenty of money (Bunny's men always come with money), her kids' favorite Uncle Freddy. Bunny sees the Life Line lasting long after the Love Line and our economic need for it has died out.

"I've canceled twice already," I continue, as if she's suggested I do it again, "but you could come with me, maybe show him your left breast."

"I'd gladly show your glamorous doctor, lump and all, but I'm sure there's a two-year wait for an initial visit," says Bunny. "It's nice to know that someone's thinking of my breast, though. Peter keeps forgetting."

Besides me, Peter is the first man she's agreed to live with, but since last week's lump discovery she's been leery. She's taken two late-night cab rides to my apartment after fighting on the phone with Peter over his lack of concern about her possible breast cancer, and though Philadelphia is not far away, it would be a very costly cab ride. I tell her she's using the lump as some sort of litmus test for love, because she's been through the breast thing before, two years ago when I was in Europe revisiting all the sights my lover and I had seen, the Eiffel Tower in Paris, the Coliseum in Rome, Harry's Bar in Venice. Bunny and I got through that breast scare with long-distance phone calls, and though it tacked a thousand dollars onto the cost of my trip, I was relieved to get her collect call in Cannes telling me it was just a cyst.

"I'll only be a few minutes," I say.

That's all it takes for my doctor to draw enough blood for a T-cell count, tiny cells that fight off infection, the AIDS virus their only nemesis. So far I've passed every T-cell test with high marks, and though Bunny seems sure that war isn't coming, I'm afraid one of these visits the battle will have begun.

"Is he near the Park?" she asks.

"Two blocks away."

"I'm coming," she moans, like the fifty-seventh second of a phone sex script, for making plans is the Life Line equivalent to mutual orgasm. The only thing left is logistics, the corner where the cab will pick her up, the market where I'll buy my meat, but Bunny lets me make these decisions, grateful I've agreed to her picnic.

■ ■ ■ ■

The cabdriver stops because I tell him to, though I wonder if he would have slowed down anyway to admire Bunny's golden hair, her tanned legs, the contrast between her sloppy white t-shirt and the polished perfection of her meticulously manicured, coral-colored nails.

"Find the fake nail," she says as she gets in the cab, her ten fingers spread out before me as though I am a manicurist. I guess the left ring finger, and she holds up her right thumb triumphantly. Bunny likes to win.

She is proud of her nails, which she stopped biting at sixteen, taking gelatin pills and painting them red as a rebellion against her no-makeup, no-money family. She has the hands of a rich woman, cold-creamed and underworked, and though her mother still says her nails look like claws, I think they suit her far more than the name Bunny does, for she is not fluffy and candy-coated. She is more like a cat, silky and soft and able to scratch, with large green eyes and tiny bowed lips. Her back is slightly arched, and though men are attracted to the felinity of her body, the curve in her spine that causes it is actually quite painful, forcing her to spend hours lying down in her dark apartment with alternate ice packs and heating pads.

"How's your back?" I ask.

"Not good," she says. "Makes me miss my government grant."

That's what we call her former boyfriend, who paid for her sometimes daily chiropractic adjustments. He was rich and ready for a second wife, but Bunny said she cared too much for him to marry for money and not enough to marry for love, so her funding was cut, leaving her to fend for herself with no health insurance, no savings account, no money.

"If Peter won't pay for it, I will," I tell her, "but you must have that lump looked at, make sure it's another cyst."

"I've already scheduled an appointment at a clinic in Philadelphia. All they do is breasts," says Bunny, crossing her arms and covering her breasts as if the lump is visible even under her baggy shirt.

"Isn't there a breast clinic in New York?" I ask as the cab pulls up to Clark's brownstone office.

"Probably, but it'll be much cheaper there," she says.

I undertip the driver, a stingy streak that comes out only in cabs. I leave 25 percent for waiters, but I begrudge tipping taxi drivers to take me from one place to another. Bunny gets out, and by the time I've carefully counted my change she is at the front door, holding down the TALK button of the brass intercom so she can answer the nurse's suspicious questions.

"It's Freddy Donovan," Bunny is saying.

"You do not sound like Freddy Donovan," says a nasal voice through the speaker. I press the button down and speak.

"Janet, it's me. Freddy."

"And a fan," adds Bunny. The door buzzes and we enter.

Except for Janet's nurse uniform, there is no evidence that there is a doctor in Clark's house. Italian tapestries are draped along the walls, concealing cabinets full of medicine. Hypodermics and hospital gowns are hidden in a large armoire. Even Janet's computer is built into the wall above her antique desk, the screen shut behind oak doors that open only when she needs information.

"Here's the star," says Janet, rising to kiss me on the cheek. It used to be the lips, and I wonder if the results of today's T-cell test will mean a hug the next time she says hello.

"I haven't been recognized once today," I say, "so my star must be fading."

"Not with your picture in every paper I read," she tells me, "even the Sunday *Times*. That hair..."

She laughs about the wig I wear in the show, a blond bouffant. I play a fashion designer, flamboyant and funny, a man who is fueled by instant espresso and co-workers' gossip. It was my idea that he have big hair that he holds whenever another character raises their voice, as if loud noises will make his hairdo fall, like a baking cake. Bunny's hobby is hair, having long been in charge of cutting mine, so I got her hired as the hair consultant, program credit and all. I liked having her at the theatre every night, enveloped in a cloud of hairspray, ratting and teasing as we talked, taping the laced front hairline to my skin and burying a microphone the size of a pea in the wig's tresses so the audience can hear me even when I whisper.

I introduce Bunny as the woman behind my wig.

"Bunny?" Janet repeats, her face pinched with disdain.

"That's right," Bunny tells her. "As in hop hop hop."

"And you do hair?" she asks, a mother grilling her son's fiancée.

"Only for friends," says Bunny.

Clark appears at the top of the grand staircase, motioning me up to his office. I am somewhat nervous about leaving Bunny and Janet alone, but Bunny finds a magazine on home furnishings, hoping to redecorate Peter's house. She sits at the other end of the room from Janet's desk, next to the French doors that look out onto Clark's garden.

His office smells like a men's club, wood and leather. The decor is mostly English manor, with a touch of midtown restaurant: photos of Clark with his well-known patients, for he is Physician to the Stars.

He's been mine for fifteen years, since I worked as a waiter at an Upper East Side cafe where several customers commented on my resemblance to their doctor. I had just moved to New York, so when I woke up one morning with a high fever and low energy, I had no one to call. I remembered Clark's name, looking him up in the phone book and begging the overprotective Janet for an appointment. Clark got on the line, and as soon as I said I was new to the City, he agreed to see me. Neither of us thought we looked alike, but Clark made me feel better, charging me fifteen dollars and offering me five back for cab fare home. I didn't take it, walking from the shade of his tree-lined street back to the heat of Hell's Kitchen, slightly dizzy from fever but buoyed by the hope that I had a future as one of Clark's famous clients.

Clark sits across a large mahogany desk, waiting for me to speak, and I confess as if he's a kindly priest.

"I know eight months have passed since my last three-month exam."

"Time flies when you're having fun," he says, lifting one of the most glowing reviews from my file, which lies open on his desk, years of lab reports, Christmas cards, newspaper clippings. Clark holds the review like a proud father, and though I'm wearing my wig in the picture, I see the resemblance between us: long faces, big teeth, square smiles. "How long do you think you'll run?" he asks.

I shrug. "There's no way of knowing. Six months, a year ... as long as people buy tickets."

Clark pulls the examining table down from the wall, like a Murphy bed. I sit on the rickety table, my feet dangling over the edge. I am over six feet tall, and this is the only seat left from which my feet don't touch the ground. Clark stands behind me, pressing his fingers into the back of my neck.

"If you ever grow tired of medicine, you could make a fortune as a masseuse," I tell him.

"Masseur," he corrects me, searching for swollen glands. His hands are on my shoulders, a perfect phone-sex scenario, though Bunny would have me out of here in sixty seconds, tossing a pithy parting line about needing my prescription refilled regularly.

The tapes are recorded in a state-of-the-art studio, with headsets, playbacks, and an engineer who does this part-time to support his painting. It is hardly an erotic environment: even the requisite slurping sounds are made by sucking my thumb. Bunny can't believe that men are actually turned on by these tapes, but sometimes late at night, I call, and though I cringe at the sound of my voice on TV interviews or radio spots, barely able to identify it as my own, I like my Love Line voice, knowing it arouses thousands of men without frightening them, the way my touch would.

Clark takes more blood than usual, making up for missed appointments, his gloved finger pressing against my arm. I don't watch him work, studying the photos that decorate his office, interspersed with fox hunts and English flowers. There are no diplomas, no certificates on his walls, and though I know there is a family, a wife and some children, he keeps no photographs of them on his desk.

"I'll call you in a week with the results," says Clark, peeling off his disposable gloves, dropping the needle into a special receptacle.

"I prefer reviews that come out the next day," I tell him.

"Don't worry, Freddy," he says, shaking my hand. "Go live your life." He gives my hand a final squeeze, for comfort, I suppose, though perhaps it's meant as a warning, a tip from a friend telling me to enjoy myself while I can.

"And stay away from those stage-door Johnnies," he calls after me as I start down the stairs.

I turn around to tell him that with my wig they won't come knocking, but Clark is facing the wall, pushing the Murphy table back into place. It's a perfect fit, which, from this distance, doesn't look like a piece of fake paneling, and I wonder why he designed this nonclinical set, then costumed himself in a lab coat.

His house is cool and quiet, the faint hum of a hidden air conditioner, classical music from a hidden speaker. Even my footsteps are silent on the thickly cushioned carpet, but as I reach the bottom of the stairs, I hear tense voices.

"I'm Freddy's best friend," Bunny is saying.

"Unless you're a patient of the Doctor's I can't help you," says Janet.

I am stopped on the landing, imagining Bunny's bra undone, her hand feeling her small breast to locate the lump for Janet, when I hear Bunny whine from the waiting room, "My back is throbbing..."

"See your doctor."

"I don't have one," Bunny says, and I can tell by her voice that she's tired of being nobody's patient. "I'm only asking for aspirin."

"Our policy is the same for prescription and nonprescription drugs," says Janet, seated at her desk and preparing my bill in perfect penmanship. Bunny's back is turned, her hands holding the painful spot in her spine where it sways in at her tiny waist. She is facing Clark's garden, probably identifying the colors in each flower, for she prides herself on knowing the name of every hue, able to distinguish sapphire from navy from midnight blue.

Janet notices me in the doorway.

"Do we need to see you again soon?" she asks, flipping Clark's appointment book a few months into the future.

Bunny turns around. "I hope not," she says, and though I know she is referring to my health, Janet is offended, a flustered hostess waiting for her rude guest to leave. I suppress a smile at Janet's hurried processing of my bill, the loud stamp of Clark's signature onto my insurance form sounding like a judge's gavel, but Bunny's face is weary from back pain, sullen with defeat over the aspirin issue.

This is not a look she wore when she came to New York to be an actress, moving into my apartment. I remember her going to my first agent's office, ignoring the large sign that warned all actors to mail in their pictures, not to phone, and above all not to knock on the locked office door. Bunny knocked anyway, first lightly and using my name, then loudly and screaming my name, then kicking the door until it was dented. Finally the agent opened the damaged door, taking her picture and dropping me as a client. Soon after that, Bunny abandoned her acting career to stay home and write, but it took me over a year to get another agent, and though I was angry at the time, I'm now inspired by the image of Bunny on the other side of a door that won't open, hair gold, nails red, heels high like they used to be before her back started bothering her, when she was still capable of kicking doors down.

■ ■ ■ ■

It is as good as she said it would be, my roast beef sandwich, a bigger and later lunch than I usually eat. I like the view from this small hill: a path, a meadow, midtown Manhattan. Bunny lies beside me on the pale green grass, the angle of the incline good for her back. Her arm is outstretched toward the sky, giving it the thumbs-up sign. One eye is closed, as if she's taking aim, adjusting the position of her thumb until the late-afternoon light shines through the painted nail, illuminating the coral color so it glows like a beautiful sunset, revealing a seam where the fake nail's been fitted.

"Do you think they'll have a decent manicurist down there," she asks, "or am I making a big mistake?"

"You can always come home," I tell her.

"What about my subletter?" says Bunny. "I couldn't do that to his date book."

"To my apartment. My bed's big enough for both of us."

I remember the last time Bunny slept with me. I'd stayed at the hospital long after visiting hours were over, missing every meal, but I felt no hunger until I saw Bunny waiting outside my door holding bags of my favorite food: McDonald's hamburgers, Chinese noodles, Italian pastries. She slept in a ball at the edge of the bed, protecting herself from the flailing limbs of my fitful sleep, and by the time the phone rang soon after sunrise, I'd kicked all the covers off. Clark said it in one sentence, and after a long silence, I asked questions, quietly so as not to wake Bunny. I could hear the even breathing of her sound sleep as Clark gave me details of my lover's death, but when I turned to tell her, I was startled by streaks of blood on my sheets, searching my body in a panic, looking for a wound before I noticed Bunny's panties and realized her period had come.

She sits up suddenly, waving a tiny square tin.

"I could have stolen this aspirin," she says. "The man behind the counter was so taken with me, he wouldn't have noticed me slipping it into my pocket." She swallows two more with a swig of seltzer, celebrating what she can still get away with when men are involved, vindicated after her fight with Janet.

A beautiful brunette wearing white spandex shorts is dragged into view on the path below, jerked and whipped like a rodeo rider as she tries to hold onto the leash of her large, rust-colored puppy. Bunny squints to see if the girl is maybe a soap opera actress, or if the dog does commercials. She's constantly on the lookout for someone famous, though she won't wear her glasses in public, and in the resulting blur all black women could be Coretta Scott King, all rich women Jackie O., and any Asian, male or female, might be Yoko Ono with her new short hair. Last week she saw Tom Cruise, Tammy Faye Bakker, and J.D. Salinger at an outdoor cafe, never questioning the likelihood of those three personalities lunching together. She doesn't mind being proved wrong, laughing at how bad her eyesight has gotten, yet in the moment of recognition Bunny always trusts her vision.

"I doubt I'll spot any celebrities in Philadelphia," she says, making no attempt to turn this young woman into a star.

"You never spot them here," I say.

"But in New York, it's a possibility," says Bunny. "I'm not sure about Tammy Faye and Tom, but I swear I saw Salinger. I won't see anyone there except Peter."

The puppy frees himself from his owner, bounding up the hill toward Bunny and the beef, his leather leash trailing behind him. Bunny pets him, keeping his snout away from my sandwich as the owner orders him to come, her commands giggly and girlish, almost like a flirtation which the dog ignores. The owner hurries after him, apologizing as she grabs his leash and yanks the puppy away.

"You have to be young to wear those white shorts," says Bunny. "Thin isn't good enough."

"You've been reading too many women's magazines," I tell her.

"Peter thinks I should write for them. He's already come up with the title of my first article," she laughs, "'I Followed My Fella to Philly.'"

"Sounds like a Love Line script."

"At least I could do it under my real name."

Bunny's used a pseudonym to write the hundreds of men she has created for me, every size and shape, like a Jewish mother trying to match up her unmarried son. She thinks I disguise my voice, not recognizing the hushed whisper, the heavy breathing, and I don't tell her that I've used it before, having sex with strangers, quoting bits of Bunny's dialogue as we do it. These encounters last longer than sixty seconds, though not much, and they have the same quality as Bunny's scripts: desperation overriding desire, the way a starving man doesn't taste what he's eating when he finally is fed. Afterwards I give these men a wrong name, a wrong number, but since the show I'm afraid I'll be recognized, and I wonder what I'll do for sex when Bunny stops scripting it for me.

She is staring again, past the path and into the meadow, where a woman is walking toward us, holding hands with a boy who moves like a toddler, though he is almost as tall as the woman, and probably weighs more. As they get closer, I can see the boy is retarded, and though his features are distorted, his eyes magnified by thick lenses, he looks like her, with the same wiry red hair and newspaper-print sort of pallor. The woman reminds me of a puppeteer maneuvering a marionette, her arm dropping down when the boy's legs lurch forward, jolting up when his knees give out.

They are near enough now for Bunny to know they're not famous, but still she watches them.

"I couldn't do that," she says.

"You could if it were your son," I tell her.

"Physically I couldn't," says Bunny, "not with my back. I'll barely be able to lift my own baby, and, Freddy, worst-case scenario: this lump might mean no breast-feeding."

Her eyes fill with tears, for it might also mean no breast. I put my arm around her shoulder, which feels tiny and frail to me: I am accustomed to the broad shoulders of a man. Bunny and I are not physically affectionate with each other, though we were when we first met, lying on her narrow bed long after her parents turned out their light, trying not to wake them with our laughter. Sometimes we'd fall asleep and I'd stay the night, having morning coffee with her parents, then going home to mine, but once I awoke when it was still dark and saw the moon sitting right outside Bunny's window, shining into her room like a searchlight. Gently I stroked her arm, from the tips of her glossy nails to her slender shoulder until she opened her eyes, and even then I did not stop, unbuttoning her blouse, unzipping her jeans, undressing her completely before we'd even kissed. I made love to her in the moonlight, and though she must have found me inadequate and inexperienced with women, my memories of that night are warm and soft and moist, and I've always suspected that's why she did it: letting me love a woman so I would feel more like a man.

The woman and the boy are stopped on the other side of the path, standing on the edge as if it is a river they cannot cross. She leans down, saying something to him, and together they leap, landing at the bottom of our hill, which is hardly steep. Still, the boy has great difficulty climbing it, holding onto both the woman's hands, her bony forearms reminding me of the cords that mountain climbers use: thin steel lines that are strong enough to save a life. I'm trying not to stare, looking past them into the distance of the dazzling skyline that surrounds the Park, when I realize I am being stared at.

"My son and I saw your play," says the woman, slightly winded, then as if to explain, "I take him to everything with music and color."

"Must have money," Bunny whispers so the woman won't hear, though she is several feet away.

"Did you like it?" I call to the boy. I'm not sure if he understands me, but he moves closer, and I squeeze Bunny's shoulder, for she is barely breathing, unable to speak now that she clearly sees this boy, whose body can't stop twitching and jerking, his head lolling back as if the slope of this tiny hill is making him dizzy.

"We loved it," the mother answers for him. "Thank you." She tells her son to wave good-bye, dropping his hands as if waving's the one trick she's taught him. I shake my palms and Bunny wiggles her fingers, and I think of how her gleaming nails must look to the boy, shiny and bright like brand-new toys.

But the boy is looking at me, and though his hands are high over his head, he is not waving. He is reaching toward my face, and when his mother coaxes him to continue up the hill, he makes a sound like an oxygen machine, an "h" stuck in the back of his throat. To him it is obviously a word, though not even his mother can understand it.

"I think he really does recognize you," she says, obviously pleased, though somewhat embarrassed as she tries to take hold of his hands. The boy lunges past her, his dirty hands inches away from me, again trying to speak, now sounding like someone heaving from nausea.

"What is it?" the mother asks, unable to translate, so Bunny hazards a guess.

"Hair?" she says, and the boy's body jolts at being understood, as if electrified.

"Of course," says the mother. "He doesn't understand that you were wearing a wig."

I hold my hair straight up to show him it's real. The boy opens and closes his fists, as if he wants to feel it, so I rise to my knees to be level with him. His palm is close enough for me to tell his fortune, and though his life line is long and uninterrupted, I've read that the life span of the retarded is short, yet I imagine his mother believes it will be different for her boy.

"Go ahead," Bunny tells him, standing behind me as if I'm the blank-faced wig block at the theatre waiting for her to style me, but the boy is frightened, pulling his hand away as though my hair might hurt him. The mother seems relieved to let Bunny encourage the boy, watching as Bunny rests her hands on my head to show that it's safe. I close my eyes when her sharp nails touch my scalp, their polished surface sliding smoothly through my hair like a comb.

"There's nothing to be afraid of," whispers Bunny, and though I know she is talking to the boy, I think of my test results; I think of my future. My eyes are shut so tight I'm seeing stars, not the kind that Bunny sees, but shooting sparks of orange and swirling dots of yellow. I have no sense of how close the boy's hand is, but I can feel Bunny's breast behind me, and I wonder if I were to slowly rest my head against it, would I even be able to feel the lump.

IN ANNE FRANK'S HOUSE

"I've come to Amsterdam to see Anne Frank's house," I told him. "I know I must sound like a typical tourist to you."

"I work there," Alex said, "for the Anne Frank Foundation."

"What do you do?"

"Well, in the big picture, I fight prejudice wherever it exists by keeping Anne Frank's memory alive. And in the small picture, I answer the phone and open the mail."

"Pretty small picture," I said.

Alex smiled.

Last night I was alone in my luxury hotel room in Paris, the same hotel where Mark and I stayed three years before. It seemed longer than that, a lifetime ago: Mark's lifetime. I was reading a paperback copy of *The Diary of Anne Frank*. I'd bought it that afternoon at the English bookstore along the Seine. It was the first time I'd read her diaries in almost twenty years, since fifth grade, when the other boys in my class had teased me, saying if I wanted to read a girl's diary, I should just read my own.

The men at this bar wouldn't tease me. They had all read her diaries when they were eleven and marveled at how much they had in common with her. They had all been caught putting on

Dick Scanlan

their mothers' lipstick. They had all come to Amsterdam to find handsome Dutch men who fight prejudice wherever it exists, even in fifth-grade classrooms.

"I'll take you there. Tomorrow," he said.

■ ■ ■ ■

Alex was waiting for me in front of my hotel early the next day.

"Good morning," he said, reaching out his hand and shaking mine. His hand was large and strong, like a pianist's, but his skin was soft, and it made mine feel soft too. He stopped shaking my hand, but he didn't let go of it.

He led me through the back streets of Amsterdam. It was clean and beautiful in the pale morning sun. Alex was proud of his city, pointing out houses that were built four hundred years ago, telling me stories he'd heard of the war, always holding onto my hand.

We walked through a park, stopping to talk to a set of twins in their midfifties, both with gray hair growing past their shoulders and long beards, like matching maharishis. They were sitting on folding chairs at a card table set up in the middle of the park, drinking thick, black coffee from a thermos.

"I'm taking him to Anne Frank's house," Alex told them.

They had gentle smiles. Alex told me they never forgot a face.

"When you return to Amsterdam, even if ten years have passed, they will know you."

■ ■ ■ ■

"It looks closed," I said, standing in front of the Anne Frank house, suddenly afraid of it, as if it were haunted.

"It is closed," Alex said. "You're getting a private tour. We have an hour before it opens to the public."

He rang the night bell, and an old man cracked the front door open. Alex said something to him in Dutch, and the old man let us in. The house was silent, and I became aware of Alex's breathing behind me as we climbed the steep stairs.

The old man swung open the bookcase that hid the entrance to the Secret Annex, but he stayed behind as Alex and I entered. The rooms seemed tiny, as childhood places do when you return to them as an adult. Her bedroom walls were covered with pictures of movie stars, still smiling. I thought of the posters that hang in my old bedroom at my parents' house, the ones that watched over me during my childhood, and still keep an eye on me when I go back for my yearly visit.

Alex led me upstairs, into the room where Anne fell in love with Peter Van Daan. It was much brighter than the rooms below, with clear, yellow sun streaming through a large window. Alex took hold of my other hand and pulled me to him, kissing me, gently at first, then passionately, then biting my lower lip as he unbuttoned my shirt.

"Can anyone see us?" I asked.

"It's a hiding place, remember?" he laughed.

We made love on the floor, not on the bed. I pretended he was my first lover. I pretended we had to stay there forever, clinging to each other to survive. I pretended he had never done this before.

The old man shouted from downstairs.

"The house opens in five minutes," Alex whispered.

We put on our clothes, which were sprawled around the room.

"Are you sure you have everything?" he asked, kissing the palm of my hand.

"Yes," I answered, but I felt like I was leaving something behind, something that belonged there. I grabbed Alex's broad shoulders and wrapped his arms around me, smelling his warm morning smell and looking beyond him, through the large window, at Anne Frank's view of the world: a chestnut tree; past that, a church tower; past that, the sky.